The Canvas

A Secret From The Holocaust

Eveline Horelle Dailey

The Canvas

A Secret From The Holocaust

Eveline Horelle Dailey

The Canvas – A Secret from the Holocaust

Eveline Horelle Dailey

The characters portrayed in this novel are products of the author's imagination. The stories are based on the lives of people she met. History of the Holocaust has been respected. The group of numbers as indicated on one arm is not one of archives.

For information contact the author at: evelinenow@gmail.com

Cover Design by: Ravit Solomon – Born in Jerusalem of families from Poland and Morocco. She is a graphic artist, contact her at: <reese89@gmail.com>

Photo: Dean Isenberger

Editing: Gretta Bishop - Doris Solbridg

Preface: Copyrighted Poem by Donald Thomas Dailey *The Grand Canyon Speaks*

Evelinenow@gmail.com - www.evelinenow.com

The author has made every effort to ensure the accuracy and completeness of information contained in this book. The intention of the author is to remind the reader of consequences of war.

Library of Congress No. 1-671686181

ISBN 13- 978-0-615-55352-8

The Canvas is dedicated to

Daphne Mc Guffie-Rafizadeh

Rachel Mc Guffie-Emigh

Sedona Emigh

Contents

Preface

It appears to be evident, how we think, what we think of and how we act potentially can change the world. Not too long ago, a thought almost did.

Words I could have written as a preface gave way to the following poem.

The Grand Canyon Speaks

By Donald T. Dailey

Man walks to my edge

And silently stares

Pauses a moment

Then his voice fills the air…

Beautiful, glorious, grand and divine

Then he humbly mutters

How insignificant his life is to mine.

Slowly he turns

And walks away

Not hearing my words as I say….

Eveline Horelle Dailey

Man, you are the wonder of this land

The greatest expression of the master's hand...

Only wind, rain and time can change a canyon's face

But man, with a thought, can change the human race....

Can I leave my readers with seeds to grow a better world?

Acknowledgements

I wrote *The Canvas* because I felt compelled to. A young woman noted a secret in the story and created the cover. Because of Ravit Solomon *A Secret from the Holocaust* became part of the title. I thank her for her vision.

It took stories I heard, life experiences of many who survived the Holocaust to infuse me with something that burned inside. The exploration into many lives, feelings about war in general are at the core of this story. For me it became a life-changing centerpiece. The burning sensation gave way to feelings of love, compassion and acceptance... the stuff remembering is made of!

I thank my parents, Isabel and Edouard Horelle, who polished the grain of sand that I was. I am grateful to Suni Paprotta and her sister Wiltrude for allowing me to read in their translated form documents kept for decades. In Wiltrude's memoir (1932 to 1956) I read about Uncle Jacob. I understood fear, sorrow and the shame of those who were not Jews and of those who were.

An older woman showed me a tattoo, all black numbers on her wrinkled skin. When she saw tears welling in my eyes, she said, "Dear, you must learn about acceptance. There are things you cannot change. Do what you can, the best you can with your book and never forget." Mrs. O. did not give me her full name. "That is not important," she said.

Numerous people have opened doors for me. I give special thanks to Wayne Strong, Frank Densmore, Jim Dusiek, and many more for their stories and perspectives based on personal experiences during WWII.

I thank Susan Friedman Kramer for her friendship, support, and inspiration, for telling me about her friends, about Auschwitz and love found in such places. With Mrs. Claudine Hattaway, I celebrate new friendship and thank her for allowing me to read about her parents. To my brother/hero, Guy Horelle, I give thanks for his stories, information about our own family, and what could be found at Yad Vashem. Merci Guy!

To those responsible for the information kept at Yad Vashem I owe a debt of gratitude not only for what I found but also for accepting my book in their library.

Mrs. Gerda Klein had encouraging words when I told her I was writing a story influenced by the Holocaust. I also thank her publicly for the signed books to my granddaughter Sedona. Susan O'Neal, I single you out for the introduction.

I thank my husband Donald T. Dailey for the use of his poem and for his words and wisdom.

The Canvas

Only the universe can answer why Dena Beth Jaffe, from a temple I did not know, came into my life. She extended her hand, offered support, and introduced me to more survivors.

A song by Leonard Cohen "The Partisan" is also responsible for the fiery emotion I felt when writing about some who changed their identities, lost wives, husbands and children. Other inspirations came from my memories Tante Denise Siegel and her family, cousins no longer alive.

As I write these words I realize I should name many more who are held in my heart and mind. So many — so much gratitude.

Eveline Horelle Dailey

Introduction

The adults around me talked about W A R —— I was too young to understand the word. There was movement and almost inaudible voices of people in darkness of night. They talked about Jews, I did not know that word either.

I am not a Jew, but the stories I heard about the Holocaust never left my mind.

One day, when I was talking with a group of people about my first book, *Lessons from the Lakeside,* one man asked, "What are you working on next?" I told him it was a book using the Holocaust as the backdrop, a human story of great love and discoveries. Another person asked me, "Why the Holocaust, what's it to you? Are you Jewish?"

I paused a moment and heard my voice, " I am not a Jew, I was not there, but I remembered stories I heard. They instilled in me a need to know more and a greater need to tell others. With respect and love I will unfold the story of two women; connected and yet differently affected by the Holocaust. Ultimately, this is something that could have happened to you or me."

Another man raised his hand, "I have something for you to read. I wrote it when I came back from the war. I was with the US Forces during WWII." A lady, frail in stature, said: "I ate bread made with flour and sawdust." These people trusted their instinct and felt it necessary to tell me what was on their minds. I became conscious that I needed to trust my intuition and allow my pen its liberty.

Soon serendipitously, I met people who had survived one of the most horrific moments in modern history. I heard more stories. In my belly, something boiled, the mixture became acids, they disturbed my gut and they infuriated my mind. I wrote a novel interlacing events relating to that time in history... love, hope and the search for balance and identity.

I Have A Tattoo

I woke up ready to face the world. A chat with my parents about the virtues of being twenty-one did not set me free, but my long awaited gift, the key to which was in my hand was a good omen. I still did not have a car to drive but I was twenty-one!

I decided to visit Suzannah; she was my shadow, my friend, nanny when I was young and confidant now that I was much older. As far back as I could remember she had always been there for me. A thousand times she said I was a blank canvas being caressed with impressions, footprints and mirages left behind by others. I have begun to understand what she meant, but no longer do I see myself as that blank canvas. Today bold colors add interest to its surface. The canvas continually changes as new brushes stroke its surface.

I had reached my majority and that was accomplishment enough! This birthday promised to be more special than anything I had ever dreamed of. The key was the assurance for the car I had been waiting for. The night before, with a group of new friends I visited a tattoo salon and treated myself. The owner was from China, I think the only one in town; he was a good artist. Wearing my brand new pair of American jeans, the black top I wore when I was fourteen but with the straps cut off, I was ready to greet the world. Strapless was my style at twenty-one —— with brilliant red lips and a head full of black curls. I left my parents satisfied with my gift but I still had to wait another three hours for delivery of my car. One quick look in the dining room mirror, I saw perfection. I had to spread the news!

Crossing the long eggshell-colored veranda flanked by tall columns, and cypresses on one side, I entered my mother's garden. The lavender scent was almost intoxicating. A few more steps and a new fragrance enveloped me, a subtle aroma of yellow irises. They were from Spain where last season Maman had purchased the bulbs. They were in full bloom for my birthday! She brought back more bulbs and cuttings every time she travelled. The garden was her love, and everyone enjoyed it. Around the corner, I entered the stone pathway leading to Suzannah's cottage. Painted an eggshell white like the main house, it had no semblance to the stately Hacienda Blanca, as mother referred to it. The cottage was very small but the same type of red clay tiles gave both roofs their Mediterranean appearance. A curve on the path, and the aroma of the yellow flowers changed. Suddenly, I was assaulted by the chemical odor of turpentine. A craftsman had just repainted Suzannah's front door after two days of sanding. The mix of Prussian and Aegean blue revealed veins within the wood I had not seen before. Perhaps at twenty-one I was becoming more aware of my surroundings. One more step and cautiously I turned the old brass knob.

Suzannah never paid attention to what I may have been doing; she just talked to me. "Since people hold the colors splashing around you, be careful because without malice or sometimes with plenty of malevolence, the colors they carry will splash you. Be mindful, Julienne, the colors are indelible. Better learn this now while you can. Twenty-one is a special time of life."

Thinking about this day brought the glowing feelings of a prior November morning a long time past. It was a few days before the assassination of the American President, John F. Kennedy, and seeing it all again in my mind's eye resulted in other realizations. The flowers, the terrazzo floor of the veranda and the almost pink flat rocks of the pathway to Suzannah's cottage belonged to another family these days. Reliving this significant period while in my new home in New England, and sitting on the porch with the two rockers, is creating the texture I could not palpate before then.

"Look Suzannah, it is my birthday! I am twenty-one years old! I have attained my majority, and I am still in one piece. I am an adult now! I will bet you never thought I would live this long! Guess what! I have a key to a car and, I have a tattoo!" I took a long breath, waiting, waiting for a reaction.

I had just finished reading two books. The first was Françoise Sagan's *Bonjour Tristesse;* I found the book interesting because Sagan's protagonist must have known first-hand about missing the mother she lost at age two. I related to her because Maman and I were always at odds. She was a disciplinarian and I

3

wanted freedom. She wanted a perfected version of me. It was important to Maman. "I will see to it that you act and behave perfectly." What I missed always was a mother who was accepting of me as I was. There was a safe arms length between us.

In books from her library I found notes from my father to her; he loved her very much I think. There were pieces of papers, old family photos and so on. Maman used anything as a bookmark. It was always a treat to find these things. When I was reading Sagan I found part of a telegram, yellow and torn and it said, —— daughter STOP arriving STOP —— I could not read the rest. Whose daughter? Arriving where? There was something about this particular note that bothered me. When I asked Maman about it, since my latest reading list did not meet with her approval, she never answered. She wanted to control what I read, who my friends were, who I talked to. Maman was difficult to say the least. The other book I read was, *Madame de Bovary* written by Gustave Flaubert, who had nothing but scandalous thoughts in his head. Great book! One day, I could be an exciting Madame de Bovary, something that would bring snow in the South of France and most assuredly the death of my mother. She felt these books were not appropriate for a young girl. She probably would have preferred if I continually read books she read to me when I was five. When I told her these books came from her library the discussion ended. We never again talked about what books I read, or their authors. It was not the time to be asked about 'daughter — arriving'. Besides, she dismissed me as she often did. I had gotten used to it but was never happy about it.

Twenty-one, so far ahead of my time! I had read literature, a few seedy books and now I had a tattoo. I had arrived!

I am amazed how sitting in a rocking chair on a porch in Maine can trigger such memories. Nothing looks or feels the same as it did when I was twenty-one, yet I am remembering. Trying perhaps to understand what Suzannah said. Attempting to understand why Maman wanted me to be not who I was but some version of her I think.

The French Riviera was at its best this fall of my birthday. A glorious day lay ahead to celebrate my birth! I was elated! The coastal town of Toulon where we resided was readying itself for the Nouveau Beaujolais delivered that very morning, no doubt in celebration of my birthday, the best day in November. The fourteenth, of course, when even the wine takes part in the celebration! How naïve I was to believe that these things happened in a country because I was born. A shipment of fish and mollusk had arrived from Marseilles; my father thought they were the finest fruit of the sea to be found in the whole of France. Our cook was busy with preparations for this evening. At the bakery, Saint-Jean, an enormous cake was being made just for me. My parents had invited guests from the world over; people my father had met and became friends with or did business with were invited for this event. The guests were well connected and according to Suzannah my father was an important man. To me, he was my Papa. I remember my mother crossing names off from the list I furnished her. Many of my friends were not appropriate, she said, her favorite terms for as long as I could remember.

My grin was broader than usual, showing off my brilliant smile. My old porcelain doll, a permanent fixture sitting between the two square pillows on my bed was no longer needed. Yet, it was not easy to give it to the servant to dispose of. Adeline was the doll's name. For years she sat on my bed, wearing her blue dress and black shoes. She too had curly hair but hers was blond. I no longer remember who gave me this doll but my concern this particular November 14 was not a doll but my jet-black hair, wild with curls. The hairdo of the day took hours to perfect. I used water and lots of sugar made into a syrupy substance to keep each curl in place. Susannah often used this concoction in my hair; she insisted it made my hair shine. Maman did not have the patience to ever comb my hair. I looked great I thought, my hair partially covering the right side of my face to give me an air of sophistication only a person of my age could understand and appreciate. My head was ever so slightly cocked to the left exactly as practiced in front of the mirror for hours, a technique developed to stress my aquiline nose. A perfect shadow of myself was cast on the wall next to the blue door. I was beaming while wearing the American jeans purchased a few weeks before at a boutique in Paris. I was in fashion and eagerly awaiting Suzannah's reaction. I still remember the wait; perhaps two minutes that seemed like hours. "Suzannah, I have a tattoo." Perhaps she had not heard me the first time.

This happened decades ago and now on this long porch, watching the harbor from my new property in New England, I can remember every detail although I am no longer twenty-one. Today is November 14, 1979 and at thirty-seven I am a widow. It is my birthday. I miss Suzannah, I miss Frank and I still question why I felt Maman envied my relation with Suzannah who was simply more accepting of me.

To My New Home

No one is ever prepared for death. I had heard these words many times before, and while I had experienced death around me, what I felt now made it all meaningless. The magic I once touched with my bare soul and body is now a series of memories wrapped in a cloak of passion, laughter and sorrow. These days, I am allowing life to take me where it will. Time has gone by. I have not succumbed to fear but while in the process of experiencing this great love, immersed in life's fleeting moments I had not prepared my self for a life lived on its own terms. Frank did that well and his essence is teaching me about life's engagements. Something radiates within me whenever I think of this man!

He was born in Massachusetts and promised me we would visit and perhaps move to the United States after his retirement from his post at the Sorbonne where he taught American Literature. He was fifty-seven when we married. A simple ceremony with friends and my mother in attendance was all we needed to become husband and wife. We had a great dinner at home, compliments of his student body. Our little apartment was bursting with pure bliss. Mother did not understand this American in Paris, but she liked him nonetheless. Perhaps his age and position had something to do with it. She thought he would harness the wild side of me. When she arrived in Paris, two days before the wedding, she was surprisingly casual in her approach. "Now Julienne, this man is appropriate for you. He seems stable though he must be a bit of a Bohemian. Why did he leave his own country to come to Paris?"

Had the two met, my father would have said he was a man of character and I think they would have liked one another. Suzannah would have insinuated that she was pleased. She would add, I was adding the colors my canvas needed and this man in my life had a good brush.

My sorrows no longer paralyzed me, the experience was sublime, and I grew to understand better what life was all about though I still had plenty of unanswered questions. I was mentally revisiting our residence in Paris; the apartment on the third floor from the side entrance of a magnificent bookstore called the Librarie Frost where we met. Among others they sold books by American writers and poets in their translated versions.

I was at a reading area of the library with volumes of Emily Dickinson, e.e. Cummings, Robert Frost, Edgar Allan Poe; American authors translated to French which I hoped to read before taking a class. This charming man walked up to me. When I looked at him I noticed his eyes were neither green nor blue, but more an amber color, I thought of the eye colors many people of Afghanistan seem to have. He coughed, and stepped closer. He wore beige corduroy trousers and his shirt woven in a pencil-striped pattern was deep green. His jacket was a camel hair color and looked Italian; it proved to be a perfect fit on his six-foot plus frame. This man had shoulders I could rest my head against.

"My name is Frank Fairchild," he said. "I see you have selected authors from where I was born. May I join you?" He did not give me time to reply as he picked up the books I had placed on the seat next to me. He sat down holding my books on his lap. "Do you like the New England area or is it American writers and poets you like?"

No need for formalities here, "My name is Julienne Duprée." I told him. "I have never been to New England and I have never read an American writer but I am about to sign up for a class at the Sorbonne where I intend to study American Literature."

He smiled in a way that strongly attracted me. "This is your lucky day, Mademoiselle, because I will be your instructor."

Without giving me notice, he put the books on an empty table next to a bookshelf, produced a piece of paper from his jacket and scribbled something I could not read. Placing the paper on top of my pile of books, he offered me his hand. I took it without a thought and he escorted me out of the store.

Keeping pace with him, and feeling rather good, I was comfortable on his arm. For a while we did not say a word; I think we were both trying to understand what we were feeling.

We walked the three blocks to the Sorbonne, where I registered and then we continued to a café. Over café au lait and a brioche, we continued our now lively conversation that did not stop until his last day. We had four days together before classes began. I still smile and feel a vague stirring when I summon these memories. Every establishment of the Latin Quarter was, according to Frank the most unique place he had ever seen.

Each open door gave us reason to stop. Frank also seemed to have known every merchant, every café and talked to every passerby. He was different from anyone I had ever met, and also older. It was late in the day when he suggested we should go to my apartment pick up a change of clothes. We had a few days before classes and we were going to be together.

Somehow, this man, without effort, managed to whisk me off without disturbing a feather. I was bound to a place I did not know. I cannot say the winds of love blew under my wings; it was not love at first sight although it held a hint of destiny. We became friends in an instant, lovers in less than twelve hours, husband and wife in less than thirty days.

This is how my journey to America began. My beloved Frank did not accompany me; instead, he succumbed to lung cancer. The vibrancy of life this man exhibited with me, his students and others, did not suffice to combat this lethal opponent. I was left with memories of him in our little apartment, and the key to a home he had purchased in New England in a town called Bar Harbor in Maine. That key summonsed feelings I had when I got my first car. Maman thought I was going to kill myself driving while I wanted wind on my face. From the map he showed me, and the stories he told me about the area I knew it would be different from Paris or any other place I had visited. Frank purchased this nest as he called it, after a real estate agent he knew mailed him two photographs. I never met this person, at least not yet. Getting to know Frank took no time at all and I understood why it did not take him long to become my husband. He told me stories about New England, its early beginning, the historical figures in America and their quest for freedom.

I learned about the climate but he did not tell me how frequently it changed. I could even visualize the people. Had he survived, it was where we hoped to move one day. Frank had no difficulties talking about life and death, reminding me often of the impermanency of things and life itself. "Julienne, we are born to die." This was something I did not care to hear.

While the cancer was ravaging his body, Frank asked me to continue with the classes at the Sorbonne. "Julienne, if you had not met me you would be in school opening your mind to new worlds, formulating and molding the new you. Do not stop going because I am in bed. Your repertoire of stories every day will bring me what I love. Do not deprive me." Off to school I went, and everyday I had something new to report. I was not a great cook, so often I stopped and bought breads, cheeses and the salami he loved. He could no longer have a glass of wine or a cup of coffee. Instead, we drank various mineral waters, and ate lots of marmalades because his taste buds were affected by the medicines he took. Sweets were still acceptable. To this day, I still drink mineral water, but no longer do my lips touch marmalade.

I had been restless a while, thinking of things we could have done, the child I never had, Suzannah, Maman and Papa all no longer in my life, and now Frank. Unhappy about my existence as it was, I decided to move to the USA. This was a decision requiring deliberate thought. I was contemplating moving to a new continent, where I knew no one and did not speak the language well. I wanted to be where Frank had been.

A great amount of international documentation had to exchange hands between groups of lawyers before the home became officially and legally mine.

I felt I had unresolved abandonment issues in my life. I had to face my father's death. After dealing with this, it was my beloved Suzannah who left our home in the South of France for a place in the Dominican Republic where she had friends. The fact that mother had requested it did not matter to me. I felt betrayed by Maman and abandoned by Suzannah. A change of country and scenery would do me good. At times the decision terrified me but I also felt a pull toward this new adventure. The thought of experiencing America as Frank had would give strength to my memories of him. Personally experiencing the things he had told me about, like going to antique stores, bookstores, museums, and much more was important to me. I vowed to walk the harbor with him in my heart. The desire to visit the places Frank had promised to take me was imperative to my recovery and growth. The journey into Frank's world would include the homes of American writers and the museums he loved in various cities and states. The idea was to spend a year travelling. After a period, I would settle and find something to do, perhaps teach French at the university. There was no immediate need to speculate; it was too early.

I no longer recall how long this voyage took. I had to ship to this new place all the things I had accumulated and now all treasures to me. This new address, however mysterious, was full of promise.

In Paris, all of my belongings were stored, and I was handling the family business affairs in Toulon. My mother had died suddenly of a stroke, and, in a way I am glad she left this world quickly. I was there that day, stoic as ever but she could not talk, it was only four months after Frank's death, and I was not ready for that. Selling the family home was essential to my recovery; I wanted no strings if a continental change was in the cards. I had no reasons to keep the house and there were no heirs. The last day there, in a surreal state, I walked through each room of Hacienda Blanca. The gardens were no longer magical and the place no longer held my heart. The glue that held my world together was gone.

It was a long voyage, from the Lyon Saint-Exupéry Airport then Orly in Paris to my final destination, the Bangor International Airport in the United States. I felt I had lost a year. I will probably always remember how eventful this journey was and how it changed my life. I came to realize I was not mentally prepared for the decision I had made. I was apprehensive, and the unknown did not hold the air of adventure it had before boarding an airplane. What I searched for did not seem to be at the end of a runway. There were two stops during this long voyage, one in London, with was a two-hour layover. During the long wait I gave some serious thought to going back home. Alas, I no longer had a home to go to in France. I boarded the plane to the USA with mixed sentiments. Things were not what I wanted them to be. Loneliness was not the feeling I had anticipated when we first talked about going to the United States. The plane was filled to capacity, I was on edge, I could not read or sleep and after hours of torment, there was an unscheduled stop in Philadelphia because something was mechanically wrong with the plane. All passengers had to get off the plane and wait for the right connections. Had this been a New York stop, for certain I would have disembarked and spent a few days visiting Manhattan. During my three-hour wait, I roamed the airport's corridors. I attempted my first American hot dog. Frank had told me about ball games and eating these things. After the first bite I knew they would never become part of my diet. The corridors were wide enough and people were everywhere. The greater disturbance had to do with attempting to understand the rapid staccato of the various tongues. A diminutive store between a coffee shop and a small restaurant selling more hot dogs caught my eye. This is where I purchased a map of the USA and one of Maine. The map of Maine was yellow with age but contained the information I needed. Leaving the little store in a better mood, I found a corner where I could spread my map and my spot was not too far from my departure gate. The universe was good to me I thought, as I opened my aged map.

I concluded I would have about a two-hour drive to my home. Realizing this, I very nearly panicked. I was not feeling at home at the airport, I did not understand the signs and had to refer to my pocket dictionary in order to communicate. Driving alone in the middle of the night was not conducive to confidence.

After two hours had passed, we were informed it would take another hour. During this merciless wait I studied every square centimeter of the map.

We landed five hours late. Exhausted, I had to find transportation to take me to my address and this was problematic. The travel agent had taken care of everything, I thought, except the car rental. The agent was wonderful, showing me where I was on the map and where I was going. A young porter, transporting my two suitcases, followed me like a young dog. I hoped with the aid of my road map I would find my home, much later than anticipated but at least I would find it. As I walked toward the cars I remembered I had to locate the telephone company to announce my arrival to someone. The telephone connection details had been handled by my agent in Paris, but I wanted to be certain

17

communication would be available to me in my home. The young man with my luggage, pointed me to a series of public telephones. My billfold contained currency but no coins. Jack was the name on his tag, so I asked Jack if he would exchange some dollars for me. I do not think he understood my jargon, but, with a smile, he handed me a coin, telling me it was a quarter. Puzzled, I asked him a quarter of what? We had an incomprehensible exchange, and finally pulling out a few more coins out of his pocket he explained their denominations. "This one is a dime, there are ten of those to each dollar. Four like the quarter I gave you also made a dollar and, this one is called a penny. You do not want to pay anything with pennies because it takes a hundred of them to make a dollar. Sorry I do not have a nickel." We both laughed when I told him I would hire him to become my banker and my English teacher. I think he understood me. I explained as best I could, I needed to call the telephone company and announce I had arrived and I wanted my telephone connected as soon as possible. Without hesitation, "Mam, they are closed now, you'll have to do this tomorrow."

The reasonable decision was to deal with the telephone matter in the morning. I had learned to cope with the death of my father, with missing Suzannah and I also missed my mother. Without Frank, I felt lost but I was fine. I could wait for the telephone.

Jack brought me back to reality. He pointed to my car. It was a black Chevrolet the size of Noah's ark. He put the suitcases in the trunk; it was about the size of our Paris kitchen. I gave Jack a kiss on each cheek which caused him to blush, but he recovered right away when I gave him two twenty dollar bills. The exchange between Francs and Dollars was still a mystery to me.

Once in the car, with my maps open on the passenger seat, I began the drive without a clue as to how long it would take to find what Frank called *The Next*. On my map from the rental company I found US Route 1, but could not see where Owl's Head was. It was in this miniscule locality I would find the address, and recognize the house in the dark — a house I had only seen in an old and torn photo. For reasons I did not understand Frank did not have a full picture of this house. I knew he had the place painted eggshell white because I had told him stories about my childhood residence. I suspected he never thought of having pictures taken. The absent-minded professor! He did not get a chance to visit Toulon. He would have liked it there, and the chance to be here with me tonight was also not in the cards for us.

I kept on driving at a slow crawl. Looking for a house facing the harbor. Because of the time spent waiting to embark after the fiasco of mechanical problems, it was too dark to see much and I could not tell the colors of the houses I passed. They all faced the harbor, they all had trees behind and in front of them. Still none of the ones I could see had a porch or I could not see any thing resembling a porch anywhere. The harbor was barely visible. I was about to cross a bridge when I stopped to check the map. All was in

19

order except how I felt. I was driving in the right direction, at least ten miles under the speed limit, which was unusual for me. Until this very night, I always thought driving was to be done at optimum speed. As a few lights appeared I looked for a freshly painted house I could not see. The torn picture with its long porch was my only clue. It was dark I was frustrated, scared and very tired. Suddenly, as if waking from a dream, I realized I would not be able to see my house because there would be no light on to illuminate it. Again I stopped, visually shaking this time, retracing my route and what I had seen: driveways, names I could not read, nailed on trees trunks and poles, very few numbers on low signs. I took a deep breath; I had not yet passed one with our name, I was almost certain.

I was too tired to think but panic was setting in with each mile I drove, and I was totally exhausted. There were no streetlights, too few stars above and only a sliver of a moon. I had gone twenty-four hours without sleep. Tears now rolled down my face as I prayed for better night vision. At last, to the left and low to the ground, an illuminated sign became visible, possibly eggshell white, with dark numbers. The sign was framed in what could have been the deepest blue my eyes could distinguish, I read *Fairchild*. I stopped the car and this time my tears were tears of joy. I had made it to my new home in America!

I still can recall the fear and the sorrow I experienced that night. I felt completely spent and wondered how my friend Suzannah could have survived her journey through life. I continue to taste the joy I felt when I saw the bold FAIRCHILD. The appearance of a simple sign within my line of vision had changed something within but I was still crying and I was still petrified.

The House in Maine

It was after two in the morning when I noticed the sign. In order to drive through, I had to open a wooden gate held by two rather large columns. It was dark, and I decided not to close the gate. If there was a fence I could not see it. Aside from my headlights there was no light. I could see as far as the beam would illuminate and no further. I drove what I now know were only minutes. Even so, with every turn of my wheels the elements of doubt mixed with other feelings made the curved driveway seemingly endless. I had to believe I was on the right path going to the right house; it said so on the sign. My mind knew the name and the address, my hands were sweating and I could feel tremors up and down my spine. There was also something ethereal and frightening about being in total darkness. I had never experienced anything of the kind. Not knowing what I would find, I could now feel my accelerating heart about to jump out of my chest.

I drove slower than when I was looking for the address. At one point a motion detector light came on. A miracle! I may have been holding my breath because with the light came a deep exhalation. I could see a white house, and a porch that seemed suspended. My headlights had already traced a circular driveway. I did not see a garage. I parked the car several feet away from the steps leading to the porch. The front door was blue. Somehow I could tell. I had to climb stairs with my large suitcases. I took the key out of my purse and began the climb, up one, stop, up two, three, stop catch a breath or two, up four, stop, five, six stop again and seven. The smaller of the two large suitcases had made it up the seven steps, I felt accomplished. Key in hand, I opened the front door. I was home in America.

Frank must have retained every detail of every conversation we had, the front door was painted a Prussian blue with a hint of the brilliance of the Aegean blue. I paused a long while. The wall switch washed the front room with light. It was too small to be called a living room, it contained two blue chairs much like the ones Suzannah had. There was a table between them, a lamp on the table, and a picture of us by the River Seine. On the other side of the room, there were two rocking chairs. I imagined this room as a reading room and with the table lamp on, I could appreciate that the chairs were covered with a fabric almost identical to Suzannah's blue chairs. Somehow Frank heard my descriptions and details. He was a conversationalist but he listened well. It was evident the two rocking chairs belonged on the porch. I turned another switch on, and this brought light to the porch. I dragged one rocker out, looked where my eyes could see. I dragged the other rocking chair out and then I sat down. I had so much to digest, all the while trying to understand how I felt. This was a moment filled with every imaginable emotion. A year has passed and I still can summons details of my arrival. It was a moment in time when I was both scared and proud of my accomplishment. I had conquered fear and found my new home. Suddenly, I felt cold. There was a slight breeze and it disturbed my dream. The remaining suitcase would not float out of the car. I had to go get it. Seven steps with a large suitcase, was like climbing Mt. Everest.

I was able to examine what I called the reading room. On the interesting table was a Tiffany lamp with a peacock design glass shade, the picture Frank must have sent to someone to put there. My two enormous suitcases were on the other side of the room. There were no pictures on the white wall.

I closed the front door, not sure if I had locked the car, but I did not care. I was too tired to be afraid or concerned.

I sat down and noticed the empty shelves. Instantly I knew every book Frank had in the apartment and some of mine would fit in their new home. Little things were giving me great pleasure including almost three walls with bookshelves. My exhaustion gave way to another feeling; I was hungry and thirsty too. I got up and headed for what I thought would be the kitchen. I found the living room and the dining room. Both were small rooms furnished with the bare essentials. Frank knew if I lived somewhere I had to give it my own identity as I had done to our apartment in Paris.

On the dining table, circa late 1800, was an envelope addressed to me in Frank's handwriting. I pulled out one of the two Queen Anne styled chair and sat down to read.

My very dear Julienne,

When I purchased this house many years ago my thought was to share it with someone special to me when I returned to the United States. You came into my life and so did cancer. If you are reading this note it is because I did not make the trip with you. I attempted as best I could to have a few pieces of furniture purchased in styles similar to those you described in your home and Suzannah's guesthouse. Sweetheart, you should have shown me pictures.

I so wanted to be with you the first time you saw the house. I am with you in spirit. My darling, know that I can live in your heart and memories. I loved you from the moment we met at the bookstore. Our life together was a short one but you made my last days worthwhile. I thank you for the gift of your love.

Since I did not know when you would visit the USA, I did not have fresh flowers for you on the table. I had two red roses put in the refrigerator by the man and his wife who will stop by when they realize you have arrived. His name is James and she is Jennifer Dillard. They have been very helpful and kind. The flowers in the fridge may no longer be alive but know they are a symbol of the love I experienced with you.

There are cans of sardines, and boxes of crackers and perhaps other things Jennifer bought. I know you must be tired, and perhaps perplexed but I think you are here because another part of your life will soon unfold. I will be with you along the way.

Welcome home sweetheart. Your loving husband

Frank.

I did not know how I would survive the emotions I felt. Still hungry, I went to the kitchen. In the refrigerator I found the two roses, along with a bottle of mineral water, and in the freezer, a baguette. Three cans of sardines in olive oil from Portugal were on the counter. As always, Frank had thought about what I liked. I wondered about the man and woman he had mentioned. I saw no signs of life when driving in. As I broke off a piece of frozen bread, I wondered how they would know I had arrived since I did not have a telephone to call them.

The mixture of excitement and sorrow gave way to a new feeling — the awareness and the fact that I was exhausted and needed to sleep. Everything else would have to wait. I did not open a can of sardines but I had a piece of frozen bread and some Perrier. I thought of stories Suzannah had told about war and no food, the idea made my frozen bread taste better. Heading toward the hallway I saw three doors. I opened the first one, a room with an easel and chair facing a large window. I smiled, as I had told Frank I wanted to resume painting. My creative endeavors had stopped when Frank became too sick to take care of himself. I missed his hand touching my face. His eyes very pale toward the end could still bore into me. His voice, when not expected could still say something to make me laugh. "Laughter, Sweetheart, you must always have plenty of that." I missed his voice. He was not there and we could not discover anything together. Alone, I walked to the second door. A bathroom with a tub with clawed feet stood still; the walls were pale green. The other door led to yet another bedroom, that one contained no furniture but a picture I think of the harbor. The house was larger than I had imagined. The hallway turned and led me to another door, this time it was my room with a very large window facing what appeared to have been a garden. It was too dark to tell. There were two other doors left unexplored as I tried to look out. One door was an adjourning bathroom; I felt privileged. This area of the house was neither blue nor green, but rather a sage color applied not with a brush but a sponge. I could tell the walls were once white. I liked the finish, a bit amateurish, but done with care. I wondered if Frank had something to do with the finish. I had a wall in Paris with similar colors and finish. I would make a point of asking James and Jennifer when I met them. As care takers they would know these things.

I turned and on the bed that was not made I saw two square pillows and them between, a porcelain doll. She looked

28

similar to the one on my bed for twenty-one years. Without undressing or looking anywhere for sheets, I sat on the bed and held my doll. I must have I cried myself to sleep. There was a knock on the door. I saw no clock nor did I have my watch on, it was daylight. In my poor English, I asked who it was, and a female voice answered "Jennifer and James" I asked them to wait. The woman sounded pleasant and happy and the man said nothing.

After splashing cold water on my face to wake me up, I shook my head, fluffed my curls, and looked at myself into the mirror I had not noticed the night before. I was relieved to see that my dress did not look slept in. I walked down the hall to the library, it was more than a reading room. I opened the front door for my first guests.

The couple knew there was no coffee; they brought me coffee and cream in a paper cup, bread with cinnamon and raisin, it was already sliced and I had never seen this type of bread. I smiled, and thanked them as I reminded myself I was in a foreign country and everything including the food would be different. There was also butter and a quarter wheel of Brie in this care package. I almost felt at home. They gave me a wonderful bouquet of wild flowers. Jennifer told me they came from the backyard. She was talking about the garden I could not see from the master bedroom. I made a mental note to explore this garden later on. I told my new friends I had a great deal to discover, including some sort of a vase. James dashed out and came back with one they had forgotten in their car.

29

Sensing I needed time to get my bearings, they did not linger. The wife, Jennifer, was younger than I was, a petite blond with blue eyes. She wore Jeans and a T-shirt. I was not accustomed to seeing women in T-shirts with a strange design on the back. It looked washed out but it was not an old T-shirt. Her husband was average height and he, too, wore jeans also with a red plaid shirt. Frank had one of those; he called it his lumberjack shirt.

Jennifer offered me her condolences; this was a thoughtful gesture to which I did not know what to say. She took a step closer to me and gave me a piece of paper; she had written their last name Dillard. I now had a good telephone number; the one I traveled with had been changed. This reminded me I needed to handle this telephone business, when I told them James offered to take care of it for me.

Frank once told me Americans did not hug and kiss on both cheeks the way the French did. I made this discovery with Jack at the car rental place but this moment called for an accolade the way I was accustomed. They both stiffened up a bit as I kissed them, and left soon after. Much like me with the condolences perhaps, they did not know how to respond.

The coffee they brought me still warm was transferred to a porcelain cup I found in the kitchen cupboard. I went to sit on my porch, facing the harbor I could now see. The view was as different as anything else so far experienced. Eating a slice of American bread and Brie made in France, I made a mental note to put at least one table between the two rocking chairs; some plants close to the door would be nice too. For the moment I held my cup on my lap.

Many hours passed and I became aware of how peaceful I felt in my new surroundings. I was no longer crying. I think Frank knew this place would be good for me, he had hoped to be sitting beside me. For now, I needed to sort out my life and many unsettling things had to be resolved about Suzannah and also my mother. She once said my husband was so American. I wondered if Jennifer and James were thinking, "She is so French." I missed my family and my husband more than I realized. This was not a morning like any I ever had. I wished Maman could have seen my new home, perhaps she would have approved of it. I know she would have enjoyed the serenity and all the plants. Mostly, I could see myself on the porch with Suzannah. I was still angry with her because she had left our home without fighting my mother. I felt it was just too soon after my father had died but I had come to accept it. Frank suggested people did the best they could with the tools they had. Life had to go on. I was alive and had to get on with the business of being alive. I did that when I was younger and now I would use the tools I had and do the best I could. My intention was to find my place in this new society. I knew it would take time but I was determined to pursue my goal.

A shower in my new American bathroom gave me a whole new perspective on life. The bathroom even had a closet in it where I gratefully found towels. A newly constructed shower with interesting tiles probably from Italy gave this room a stately yet feminine air. I made a mental note to ask Jennifer what she knew about the tiles. The water was cold, very cold. I would ask James about changing this situation. There was also a modern and obviously new tub in this enormous room. After the cold shower I was very happy not to have thought of taking a bath. I guessed the tub with clawed feet in the other bathroom was old, but suited for the guest bathroom. It had a very clear mirror with a silver and gold colored frame. Perhaps one day I would paint something directly on the wall to frame the tub and complement the frame's intricate design. I was glad to realize I was making plans to decorate my new home. My bathroom had a mirror the width of which reminded me of a man with open arms. A series of cabinets and a sink were on the other wall I turned to examine my tattoo; it had not changed. There was a small window with a lace curtain I knew I would remove, with no neighbor across, a forest behind the house, I wanted to see out without the benefit of lace.

A Source of Exaltation – A Tattoo

Suzannah was tall and slender with incredibly long and beautiful fingers; she had clear brilliant blue-gray eyes; she was a well-proportioned woman. I had watched her hair change from a deep brown with burgundy highlights to shades of taupe and gray. She was a private person. She never mentioned her birth date or anything related to it. I did not know these things about her though she was one of the most important people in my life. I reflected on my self-centeredness as I brushed my hair. I never bothered to ask Suzannah about her age, even on my twenty-first birthday. Not proud of this behavior, I was unaware of it at that time, it was now too late to correct. If Frank and Suzannah were here with me, we could have discussed the reasons for my behavior.

Suzannah was mostly taken for granted because she demanded nothing from anyone. I adored her but was also guilty to have adopted this attitude. My mother's flower garden had that same quality. It was there to be viewed, admired, even appreciated at times, but never touched. No one touched Suzannah while she deeply touched others. Today I realize she was the most solid influence I experience. She was my teacher, my best friend, and a beloved mentor. I never told her what she meant to me, perhaps because at that time, I did not know. I treated our relationship as if she belonged to me and was eternal. Until I lost her, I never realized how important she was to me. I am discovering being young and immature was reason enough. She was kind and loving. She taught me German she spoke when she was making an important point. Italian and sciences so I would have a well rounded education she said. It is all the other things she thought me that I miss. There was always a special kind of warmth about her. When free to do so she talked with my Aunt Erika, my father's older sister, who resided in the main house with us, they were friends always talking about people and things I knew nothing about. My father said my aunt was named Erika because his father had met an Italian opera singer with that name. Aunt Erika had no resemblance to an opera singer; I found the idea amusing because to me Aunt Erika did not have the elegance necessary to be on stage. She was short and a little fat. The dresses she wore were always too short, and her large bosom seemed to always be flapping loosely from one side to the other or up and down depending of what she was doing. She wore the strangest hats and white gloves when she went out. Aunt Erika with all her strange ways brought smiles to one's face. I loved her very much but we were not close. Everyone around me kept a safe distance the cost of which was intimacy.

Frank knew the secrets to my psyche he asked questions about Suzannah, my father and mother. He met her a few days before our marriage, he liked her, but she did not understand his American ways. She was relieved I had chosen a husband, who was professor at the Sorbonne. I could almost hear her tell her friends about it. Frank would have loved Suzannah as much as I did. As his health continued to fail, sometimes he would mutter, *"I love you as much as Suzannah did."*

All the people who could possibly enlighten me about my unanswered questions are now dead; I am left with my unchartered memories and know it is up to me to extricate what I can from my mind, and examine my thoughts. If I want to know about those who surrounded me when I was young, I will have to make an effort to recall conversations and unleash what has been held hostage. If successful, the purpose of all this will reveal something hidden I am sure.

I gazed upon the various flowerbeds flanking the stone path to the front steps of my new home, not unlike the many paths of my mother's garden. The flora here is different and for some reason I am reminded of the long pauses we experienced, Suzannah and I. Frank may have had the front door of this house painted blue because he knew some of the stories I told him would be part of my self-discovery. He wanted me to have reminders and triggers. For now, Suzannah was on my mind but Frank was with me, I could feel his presence.

"You know Julienne, my eyes are not what they used to be. I must put my glasses on so I can see this masterpiece of yours. Where is this tattoo of yours?"

For an eternity I had been waiting for her response.

Promptly, I unzipped my jeans, turned, as I lowered them and showed her my butt.

"See down on the left side of my derriere, as you call it; it's the zigzagging arrow pointing downward! See, it is almost flame-colored, and hot too! What do you think Suzannah? What do you think? Is it not brilliant? I love being twenty-one! I am free, and I know it is going to be the best year of my life. I had it done yesterday. It hurts a little but only temporarily. What did you do when you turned twenty-one? I am hoping to go out tonight with my friends after my party. It will be very late. You know Maman did not invite all my friends. I am planning to have fun, lots of fun! We are all going to a new club tonight. The car will be delivered in a few hours and I will be free to go where I wish.

"I am an adult today, and a free one! Free! Suzannah, Free! Can you appreciate that? What do you know of freedom? You never go out or do the things I do."

It took a while, a long while to get her to acknowledge me. She just stood there with her glasses in her hand, one arm of the glasses resting against the right side of her mouth. She was holding the back of her chair with her left hand. She sat, looking at me.

"Julienne! Is this, the source of your great exaltation? I suppose you want me to applaud the lack of artistry and creativity. Or should I be glad you got a tattoo of a cracked arrow

36

pointing to your ass? Since you are now twenty-one, do you believe your tattoo will bring you a sense of liberty? Or is it freedom you are after? Perhaps you need to learn the meaning of the words. An arrow pointing to your ass is not a declaration of freedom. Could this be some sort of advertisement? A rebellious act against the society you refuse to fit into? I do not mean to scold you on your birthday, but I feel at twenty-one you should display respectability for your station in life and your body if nothing else. This tattoo is doing the opposite. Are you attempting a marker indicating your sexuality? Are you attempting to find your identity? Believe me, it is not your ass that will determine who you are. Far from it! I fail to understand the reason for this tattoo or its artistic worth. Meine Liebe, I do not deem this to be a display of freedom or art. Right now, I am questioning your sanity. What does your mother say about it?

Like with an automatic gun I felt attacked by Suzannah, the bullets came flying out and struck me right between the eyes.

"Julienne, there will be a time in your life when you will question your own logic. This is obviously not the time for such conjecture. But, take my word for it, one day you will question not only your sanity but you will want this ridiculous thing gone." She put her glasses on the table and nothing more needed to be said.

Until I met Frank the tattoo was never a concern. When he saw it for the first time, I was ashamed of what I had done to my body and I thought of Suzannah, and wanted this ridiculous thing gone.

The morning after we met and had made love all night long, he examined it. "I bet you believed the tattoo was going to bring you a sense of liberty and freedom. Twenty-one is a time for such insanity."

I cried in his arms that morning as the sun rose. He had not seen the tattoo the night before and now used Suzannah's words. He said one day, I would know it, and it would happen when I was ready, without fear and with resolve. Frank was so much like Suzannah. They understood the world with the same type of lucidity.

"Hold on Suzannah, you are going too fast for me, and please do not speak German to me. As I recall, you spent years telling me to express myself, so I did! I got a tattoo and it was an original thought and a free expression! It is art too! Most of my friends liked it! I am twenty-one years old and I do not need your comments or approval! In fact I do not need anybody's approval. I did not even show it to my Maman. I like my tattoo even if I cannot see it clearly. I wanted to show it to you, pure and simple."

Suzannah had a way of knowing when I needed to let out steam. I was angry, and hurt, I wanted her approval because I knew I would not get any from my mother. It was obvious she was too old to understand about being twenty-one. Perhaps in the place where she was born people did not care about anything of the kind. Farmers, and other peasants, what did they know? I did not care! I had my own life to live!

She was looking out toward the pond while I struggled with the zipper. As if to torment me, it refused to go up. She again began to talk to me.

"Secrets, intrigues, and religion are the elements that have shaped and peppered my life, and without them I would not be here letting you know about any of this. Actually, my life would have no meaning at all. Every corridor I walked, every moonlit sky I saw, every tear I shed and, every time I shook with fear are the things that prepared me. You should make every attempt to stay with balance. Not impossible, you can achieve anything you set your mind toward.

I felt the urgency to get out of her space. I was getting angrier by the second. Her lack of sensitivity and understanding were appalling. She knew nothing about art! Still struggling with the zipper I decided I would never talk to her again.

Then she continued, "In my world, ladies did not have themselves branded. If such a thing happened, it was the will of someone else. Young women did not adorn themselves with tattoos, although some men did if they belonged to pagan orders. Many indigenous cultures also decorated themselves with tattoos. Some men belonging to various orders tattooed symbols

39

on their body. You my dear, do not fit into any of these categories."

There she was, attacking me again!

"I must say my tattoo did the exact opposite. No matter how disgraceful, it at least contained history."

My zipper came unstuck; it took with it a piece of my skin. I saw the blood, but I did not care. I had to get out. Suzannah did not understand about being twenty-one. I opened the door and left. I did not slam the door, however, I wanted to. It took a minute to understand what I had heard. I was too angry to turn around and ask what was she talking about. It was early yet but I felt almost late getting dressed for my own party and my friends.

If Frank and Suzannah were here today, this very minute, what a conversation we could have! Not one about a tattoo but how we felt about our lives. Instead I was alone ready to go inside and ready myself for the company handling my boxes. I had been in the house for three days with the content of my two suitcases. The entire shipment was to be delivered this morning. Too much daydreaming had been going on. My next task would be unpacking what Frank left me to remember him by and the things from my family's home.

The truck arrived on time and made it through the driveway without difficulties. I had most boxes brought to the empty bedroom except the boxes clearly marked books, they went to the library and boxes marked kitchen went there. The two men were well compensated and left with their empty truck. I was surrounded with treasures to be discovered, one box at a time. From the kitchen, I took a long look. The visible beach and the waves were calling me. It was time to take a walk. In three days, I had gotten accustomed to the feeling of salt water on my face.

Butter from Denmark

Unpacking being rather tedious and unpleasant, I often stopped and went for long rides. Sometimes I ended up at the most wonderful shops, visited art galleries, some of which were open only a few months every year. I wondered why? Soon I saw signs to let me know winter would be difficult if people left town.

I discovered many places to purchase the things I loved. The more I drove around in my new American car, a blue Thunderbird, an appropriate name for a car for me, it went as fast as the wind but there was the question of speed limitations I was to observe. The whole of New England had a captivating charm. I was not home but I was feeling comfortable with my new surroundings. The people were courteous, not overly friendly but I was new to this environment and had to get used to differences. At an antique store I purchased an exquisite frame for my last picture of Frank showing me at his side holding two baguettes in one hand and a large piece of cheese in the other. That day some of his students were coming to break bread with us. I think they adored Frank and enjoyed the wine being poured into their glasses too often empty. There was laughter around us although we often wanted to cry. We knew every moment together was a gift and his students needed him as much as I did.

This morning's memories continue to be a mixed bag. A piece of bread with raisins and cinnamon similar to what Jennifer brought me the morning of my arrival. Now the proud owner of a toaster, I learned toasted crisp, this type of bread was good when covered with butter from Denmark. I found some at a grocer who filled his shelves with imported foods. The butter was one of my finds. Two pieces of cheese created paradise and somehow brought me back to my twenty-first birthday. It did not seem like so many years ago. I could not help but laugh, because Frank told me more than once that I knew nothing about time. My father was of the same opinion. Twenty-one, thirty-one, maybe at forty-one I would not sing a different tune. Examining the theory that a tattoo could hold something special about my personality was occupying my mind. How absurdly underdeveloped I was. And, of course, Suzannah's assessment was correct. I was a blank canvas at that time. Frank must have suspected that I was not too bright at twenty-one. Being a kind man, if he had such a notion, he kept it to himself.

I could almost see her, as if we were looking through the window of her cottage. I could touch her starched white blouse and even perceive the contours of her body the dark wool skirts always made an effort to disguise. Her lavender scent still permeates my nostrils. She made her own essential oil, but I buy my lavender soaps and oils.

I found my mind wandering much as Suzannah's did; from place to place to events unrelated to what we were talking about. A peculiar a pair we were, yet, how well we understood each other! One thought or one new word gave stories new with fertile ground to explore. Perhaps this was a way that texture was being infused into my life. It is also possible the blank canvas she called me was being prepared for the first artistic strokes. Frank told me that self-discovery took a certain amount of courage and honesty. "Know thyself Julienne. You will love you!" Like Suzannah, he was a pro at self-love and both had self-discipline coupled with determination, things I am acquiring at a slow pace.

I feel as if I am floating in a large sea in the middle of a storm. I now know I must solve the problems I have on my own. My father left me a generous sum of money and the house in Toulon sold for a fortune. Though I have thought of using the services of a psychologist, I decided not use a cent to have someone I cannot understand attempt to analyze my issues. Besides sadly enough they do not talk, they only listen. No psychiatric or psychological help for me. I am alone here, on my porch, in a rocking chair. I have all the time in the world to explore the things I have been afraid to look at and also the ones I felt guilty about. I can talk to the birds and the trees and, one of these days I will take charge of all my feelings. I will conquer what goes on inside and get a dog or two. I am told there are millions of dogs in need of homes. Two large dogs would enjoy the terrain and the harbor too. The idea of dogs brought a sense of cheerfulness. All I needed to do was to familiarize myself with the various breeds. My compilation of good memories about my life will overshadow any guilt I have about anything I can think of. As for the tattoo, I will not look at it and, for the moment there is no one to see it. The box Suzannah left for me and that I left unopened for so long will surrender its secrets. Tomorrow I will look for it! I am no longer afraid of feelings I do not understand. In one of the cartons I will find it. For now the idea of patience came to mind.

I rose from my rocking chair, feeling elated because of my resolutions. I was feeling less exasperated and exhausted from this move from one continent to the other. It was done and there was no need to ruminate over the various fears I had encountered. As I indulged in my own trauma, I could not help but wonder how Suzannah managed her life and good attitude. She was much older than I am now when she began her new life in the Caribbean. She was very young during the war that left her without family and somehow she managed all these things. How I missed her! Moving from our home by the Mediterranean Sea to the Caribbean was something that took courage. Under the same circumstances would I display such courage? What an extraordinary person! More than ever, I felt ready to open the box. I am sure if Frank had been alive he would have travelled with me to the Dominican Republic where Suzannah settled. Alas, when I got there alone, she was no longer alive.

46

She was a woman of courage; I will use her examples and follow her footsteps to conduct this new experience unfolding before me.

One of the boxes filled with books was now ready for me to tackle. The simple act of opening these cartons and placing the books in some sort of order gave me a different perspective, a sense of accomplishment. Finding small treasures tucked between layers of books gave form to my thoughts and the room. My home was getting an identity uniquely mine. Because most of the books belonged to Frank his essence was settling around me and something transformative was also in the air. I was learning about what had been hidden about him. In some of the books he had pages of papers with hand-written notes to himself. I no longer felt alone because a part of him was enveloping me. Each book I took from the box demanded that I look inside; a few pages read here and there and soon hours passed.

This library project was influencing my moods, and soon enough, I became aware in a pleasant way that conversion of this room into a library was a seven-year venture. The first box revealed Edgar Allen Poe, e.e. Cummings, Emily Dickenson, and Robert Frost. Those were the books I was going to read before taking the American Literature class at the Sorbonne. Frank had purchased them for me but never told me! They were kept in this very box in our apartment in Paris. Sometimes I used the box as a hassock, a piece of furniture we had no room for. All along the books had been with me and available to be read. I was obviously not ready and I had covered the box with my mother's mantilla. Robert Frost was ready to make its way on a shelf. A page was marked with a blank piece of paper. I looked at the paper and the page and read a poem about fire and ice, and the end of the world. I paused. Suzannah often told me the destruction of the world would not come from fire or ice but from the human race, unless we learned the art of inclusion, something she had some doubts about. What a tall order this was for my benefit on that day. The art of inclusion was not then nor now what I did best. Wondering how I could incorporate inclusion in my life left me feeling uncertain. I picked up another book and put it away without opening it. Four days had passed and only two boxes were empty, but there was no rush. Mine was a life of leisure and I liked that. This was something very new to me. With each book, I read something new. A special movement I did not know within me became a subtle caress. Soon enough, I had a routine it started with a cup of tea. Soon and with my tea, time on the porch simply watching, feeling and being. After that, time with the boxes of books and various other treasures gave way to again new feelings. I was pleased with myself. I was free of words and thoughts associated with logic. I liked my newfound freedom. I was beginning to understand an aspect of myself, I did not know.

I became conscious of a subtle change in me. When I arrived here, this type of terrace was foreign to me. I was not exactly fearful but the suspended appearance of the porch and the architecture of it seemed hazardous. The seven steps looked like they were the only things holding it together. Though I questioned the engineering, these thoughts did not keep me away even though I was more accustomed to long solid verandas made of cement with columns of granite. This was a wood construction and after examining every inch of it I knew it took a long time to build. Soon I came to realize how much love I could feel just sitting in a rocking chair on this porch. A dedicated craftsman must have taken the time to create hundreds of elongated slats and installed them one after the other. Their design may have followed a template but I could see they were individually made. Much like Suzannah's blue door, I could see tool marks on the wood grain showing under the coat of paint. The workmanship was masterful and artistic. How could Frank have known I would feel at ease here sitting in a rocker, watching the harbor and letting my mind roam to places left unvisited for too long? One thing was certain this home did fit my lifestyle. This room I baptized, as the library was perfect and ready to accept my books and his. My art and all the other treasures were finding their space. HOME! I had arrived! This place had become mine and somehow, it also held the dreams he had. His essence would carry me through places I could not yet foresee.

Like a vagabond on a holiday, my mind continued to leap uncontrollably. This was no longer a concern. I had become comfortable with myself. Random thoughts came and went of their own accord. There was no chaos, no turmoil just a steady slow flow moving a leaf to shore. Another conversation soon was ready to emerge for me to explore.

"Suzannah, did you say you have a tattoo? You are so old; I did not know people your age knew anything about tattoos. I am amazed! How old are you anyway? You better show me that tattoo of yours. What history are you talking about? You know I hate history. How come you never showed it to me, or even talked about it? And why is it you are upset because I have one too? You know, Suzannah sometimes you make no sense at all."

Twenty-one was a time to be immature and uncaring, a time for self-absorption; at least this was the way it was for me. My decision never to talk to Suzannah because she thought my tattoo was improper was a momentary pronouncement. I could not stay away from her; my curiosity had to be satisfied. I had to ask about this tattoo. I knew well I could not stay away from her.

"So! A tattoo! You have a tattoo! I cannot believe it! What is it, a pretty flower, a bird, the name of a lover, or what? Where is it? I gather it's not on your ass since you see no artistry in the placement of a tattoo in this region. Show it to me, will you! So, you were no lady —— you have a tattoo! Admit that you were once just like me. I can't believe it! You and a tattoo! Suzannah, we are so much alike! Did you belong to a gang or some other sinister organization? Did you get drunk one night and woke up with a tattoo? Is that why you did not talk about it? Are you ashamed of what you did? History you say! Well of course, every tattoo has a story to tell. Even I know that."

They got very dark as her eyes looked at me. Somehow they held their brilliance yet something somber happened. For a long time Suzannah said nothing. She just stared at me.

"You know, Julienne, you talk a mile a minute without taking the time to think. Slow down, take a moment to compose your thoughts, take a breath. Think, and learn not to say everything that pops into your head. You are twenty-one years old now; you do not need to express yourself as if you were twelve. Formulate what you intend to say seven times before you utter a word. This is a very good practice, one you may well benefit from. You complain when I speak in long drawn out sentences but I think you have the same habit. Too fast, dear child, calm down. I know life goes faster than we think but right now we are granted the occasion to talk. We are not racehorses."

"Just show me the thing, will you?" My voice was getting louder because I was impatient.

"Since you have such a profound interest and have brought this tattoo business up again, I will show you mine. I may even tell you a story or two about it. First, I must unbutton my shirtsleeve."

Eveline Horelle Dailey

A Number

Do you hear the bird? I heard him once before, a Blue Jay I was told, but he looks different from his European cousin. He was visiting the porch area yesterday, reminding me of the blue tent I had made out of cloth from Persia or Morocco that my mother did not want anymore. The blue was identical. This majestic bird caused me to wonder if all children had a kingdom under a dining table? If Jennifer has a baby, in time, I will move the chairs out and build this child a tent. In this weather, a blanket will be the appropriate material. It would have been wonderful if I still had this awesome textile at my fingertips; it had a degree of warmth. For the moment, the bird was showing me he was free; free to fly wherever he wanted and he could hide under a leaf if he wished. He was free to sing his song not to me but to himself. Life around me demanded that I become acquainted with what was around me. Frank and Suzannah had done so all their lives. They were familiar with their surroundings. Nothing was ever hidden from their view. Learning how this works is allowing me the review of my own life, pausing when I need to. Knowing what will come later was not of any importance. Frank would say, "Go with the flow. You did it when you met me."

There is no denying, I loved Suzannah and adored Frank. I never told her and it is much too late now, she died before I knew I needed to let her know. But at least by the time I met Frank I was able to express love. Left with a degree of sorrow, I am slowly shedding the guilt I felt because of my childish behavior with Suzannah. To think a life could be lived without a scratch, pretending the emptiness inside could be cured with a night of drinking or making love. It was evident the road that had taken me to this porch had also ended my escapes. Something blissful was happening.

Suzannah would have liked this corner of the globe no matter how different it was from the Mediterranean or the Caribbean. A few things went missing when I changed continent, but I am learning to adapt. I miss the bakery St. Martin, and the Fromagerie Internationale; I have not found a store here where I can buy only cheese, or only breads and pastries. I am certain I will find the things still absent in my life. The foods that are eaten here are different. What is fat has no butter and what is sweet is too sweet. Few foods seem to be in their natural state. Frank never told me about these nuances. I will explore every corner of the region and will find all the treasures and places he talked about and also the things he did not tell me about. For the moment, the trees and flowers with their unique differences and abundant large leaves were holding my interest. There are a multitude of birds residing in and around the trees. A trip to a bookstore seeking enlightenment will let me know about the various species. Looking around at the flora, I see there is no lavender here, at least not on this property.

Instead, there is a scent of mulch mixed with the aroma of flowers I cannot name. I have not noticed any of Van Gogh's sunflowers. This area may not be sunny enough, or perhaps it is not yet their season. I must acquaint myself with everything around me. Seven steps to the home and perhaps seven years to know about my immediate surroundings, my new home will make its demands and I will abide. Around beds of flowers and very large boulders I have some mums, and they give my yard the yellows I grew up with. Maybe, as seasons change, I will discover new plants. This garden, a bit wild, provides the kind of grace and elegance only nature can provide. This is not a sculptured garden as my mother insisted a garden had to be. Self-awareness and self- acceptance have become associates of mine. I do not know when all this took place. At times I feel young and vibrant, but nothing is the same. I miss the things I took for granted. I cry for Frank, I cry for Suzannah, I cry for my parents, for the good-byes I did not get to. My mind continues to flit like a butterfly from flower to flower. Per chance I feel overwhelmed by my racing thoughts, I struggle with what I know I should understand and accept. The cost of grief has caused my mind to lose its focus. I must regain the zest for life I once had. It has been long enough. With this realization comes the need for a cup of strong tea.

"How do you like that I made it! I am an adult! I reached the age of majority. Admit it Suzannah, you had your doubts! I bet you never believed I would make it to twenty-one and now I have a tattoo. I tell you I have it all, I have arrived."

The blue gray eyes, intensity followed my every move as I moved around her living room. After a long while, and without emotion she said, "Since you believe you have arrived, whatever that expression means, I will tell you a story now."

I watched her work with the buttons and realized she used a method uniquely her own. It caused me to remember the first time I took my blouse off to expose my bare breast to my inexperienced new lover. Contrary to what Suzannah was doing, I did it with passion, popping all the buttons at once. My blouse had no sleeves, thank goodness. Poor lad, he did not know what to do. We were a year apart and I was a good teacher.

A slight breeze interrupted my reverie. I watched her. Every movement of her body was deliberate. With care and concentration, she unfastened one button after the other and began with greater purpose to fold the left sleeve of her blouse. Three inches all around, perhaps a little less was folded. When finished and satisfied, slower this time, she folded her sleeve one more time and smoothed out the fold. She did this slowly, silently without creating any wrinkles. Not a word spoken, she was testing my patience, something Suzannah knew a great deal about. Her white and well-starched linen shirts all had two buttons on each cuff. Mother of pearl they were, and I swear she sewed the same buttons on every blouse. The shirts she wore were very tailored and always with long sleeves. They were almost masculine in style, and always absolutely white, freshly laundered and ironed. She was beautiful but went out of her way not to appear too feminine, although her natural beauty could not be denied. After the folding, she again looked at me, this time gravely with eyes that were moist. It seemed an eternity has passed, and then she exposed her left forearm.

"Suzannah! And you talk about the artistry of my tattoo! This is nothing but numbers 4 3 2 7 5 4."

Reflections from a Blank Canvas

I was beginning to understand and appreciate my life the way it was. When I needed to escape from my introspective journey, I took the time to visit antiques stores. They had a particular charm in this part of the world. American, German, a fair amount of Japanese and British antiques all intermingled in the same rooms. Hours would go by as I examined each interesting item. I found the storekeepers were patient and wonderful. I purchased a figurine marked OCCUPIED JAPAN; it looked like a Bavarian piece rather than Oriental. I knew nothing of being in an Occupied place. The other store I visited that morning had wonderful silver pieces and admiring them I felt as if I were in a museum. Seeing both craft and art from an early American era was a treat. On the back wall of yet another store was an exquisite handmade quilt with an intricate design executed by the hands of an expert. It hung there waiting for a patron just like me. A variety of blues and purples, whites, and greens from forest to jade formed a peacock. Somehow, the stitching and the fabrics gave the bird depth and texture. Moirés, shantung and heavy satin cloth pieces, less than a centimeter, caught my eye. This was not a simple quilt, it was a rare piece of art and it needed to be on my bed. In a curio cabinet made of maple wood that had been stained the color of honey, I found a most beautiful ivory comb. Suzannah had described one to me a long time ago. I was discovering a new me. I was joyful! I examined the comb again and for reasons I simply could not recall I knew Suzannah had made her comb a prized possession, she never showed it to me. There were few things she could not part with. I imagined this comb would have been one. How often had she warned me not to become too attached to anything I could not take with me at a moment's notice? I think the comb story had something to do with that. It was something she could grab in a rush. She would say to me when I came home with one of my finds. "And what will you do with this if you have to move? What will this treasure mean to you once you are old?" "I will take the comb." Since I already had paid for it I think the storekeeper was a bit confused. We smiled, she talked to the storeowner; they both looked at me and must have thought these foreigners, and they are strange. "In life there were times when even combing one's hair seemed unimportant." Suzannah had beautiful hair that a couple of fingers could comb. If I had to rush somewhere, I would take my comb and the quilt too. I saw the matching brush, on a different shelf, and of course I had to purchase it too. As if an ocean breeze created a constant flux every time she moved, Suzannah's hair required little care. Unfortunately, I had inherited my father's hair, too much, too thick and too curly. Maybe this is why he kept his hair so closely cropped. Sometimes, when Suzannah talked to me, I would listen while sitting in front of her mirror. On a table with a white doily, she had placed a crystal bowl centered to perfection. She never had anything out of place. In that bowl she usually had a fresh rose floating in water, just enough to release a subtle aroma. Sometimes I played with the rose or even plucked a petal or two at which point no matter where she was she would gently hit my head, "Nein!" She continued to call me a blank canvas whenever we disagreed on something, and she may have had a point. But that was then and this is now. The canvas is no longer blank.

How I wish she were here. So many fragmented memories could be clarified. If nothing else I learned from her to never wait. When I have questions or when there is something I do not understand, I ask for explanations. People died and left me hanging, searching for elusive answers.

I can see Frank looking at me. He too left me with unanswered questions I never thought to ask. All things considered, I received great gifts. My life has been one of adventure and excitement and it appears the time to reorganize is upon me. I must find my "raison d'être." If what I read in the past is correct, having a reason to be alive will propel me to my next venture. It is a fact I am seeking to shed some light on the mysteries surrounding people who have touched my life.

Frank wanted to write about his experiences in France. He told me he would begin once we were in the USA. He did not want to be influenced by French culture when he wrote about it. I will have to be attentive when I begin to go through the papers he left.

His writings, perhaps not influenced by the culture in France might have more to do with what he brought with him. I know he chose this place to retire because there were few outside disruptions, limited visible or audible traffic. This was an ideal place to sit and sort out memories or papers: an ideal place for what he wanted to do. So here I am, left alone, viewing a harbor in a continent far away from where I was born. Not completely at ease yet the very thought of the possibilities at hand are invigorating. I will take on the task of sorting through his work. Posthumous publishing is not unheard of. Because I am beginning to understand what human endurance means, and because our relationship was so close, I am the one to sort out his papers and arrange them the way he would have. I can do this!

My reveries were disturbed by a gentle breeze caressing my nostrils. The undefined aroma forced me to look at the plants in front of me. Broad leaves and flowers unfamiliar to me were dancing to a tempo I did not know. The winds here were different; the trees and other plants obstructed some of the harbor's view. I must have this taken care of. Transported once more to my mother's garden where she spent a great deal of her time, I now could understand the magic experienced. The creation of her garden held her in a trance-like state where perhaps she could find happiness. I am beginning to visit that place of hers; its name is serenity. I may never know about what was missing from her life; she did not discuss such things. I learned observing her that a spark was missing from her life. She had a good life but seemed reticent to partake in its feast. She adored her plants but her hands never touched the soil. It was Lutino the gardener with the patience of an angel who tended to this sacred place. When I walked into the middle of a seedbed, he was quick to remind me of who took care of the garden. I wondered a moment, what ever happened to Lutino —— did he return to Italy where he had family?

Maman, a medium size woman, wore pearls almost daily and now on rare occasions, I wear Maman's pearl necklace. In America they seem out of place. In her family each girl was given one when she became twenty-one. I am happy Papa had sense enough to know a car was more important to me.

I wonder why I am thinking of Maman or Lutino? She got along with Lutino because he did not engage her. Aunt Erica and I were not always able to create the mood she desired. An unspoken and unrecognized bond existed between the earth Maman and Suzannah. They were not friends but understood about gardens. They would have been very proud of me. Some changes had taken place and I even was taking care of some areas of my garden around the house. Next spring I will tackle with flowerbeds and some vegetables. The various world maps I collected did not explain the differences in the flora, and just looking about, it is evident that the leaves here are enormous while the ones in Toulon are small. Even the green takes on different shades. To my library, I will add a section that covers the plants of this region. Still thinking about dinner, I came to the conclusion Jennifer and James were very nice people. Having dinner with them would be the beginning of my American social life. From them I could learn about the people in this area and more about the language and the foods. James knew about the plants since he took care of the entire garden. He could tell me what books to get.

This geographical change with its significant differences was beginning to release secrets I felt had been kept from me. I never understood the strained relationship between Maman and Aunt Erika. I still do not know why every time I talked to my aunt Maman was upset about something. It often felt, an elephant was in the room with me but no one saw it. I may never know the answers because I have nothing here that once belonged to Aunt Erika. I rapidly decided as I made new friends these concerns would make room for other things to occupy my mind. A telephone call to Jennifer would start the ball rolling. Before another turn of my mind I was dialing. "Hello, Jennifer, this is Julienne Fairchild. I was wondering if you and James would like to come for dinner Saturday night?"

There was a pause, I could hear her voice talking to her husband I guessed. "Yes, we would love to come. What time would be OK for you?"

Not sure what to tell them because I did not know what Americans considered the normal dinner hour. I suggested they come when it was most convenient

"We can be there around 6:30 PM. I will bring a bottle of California wine."

This was a brief conversation and accomplished its purpose. I was going to have a meal prepared for my first guests, and sample wine from the country I now called home! It was Tuesday. I still had plenty of time to plan and come up with the perfect menu.

The mood change came like an ocean breeze. My new stereo in the corner of the living room was waiting to be used. The Gypsy audiocassette obliged; the music reminded me of a café we used to visit, Frank and I. Gypsies played various string instruments, and danced furiously. I, too, danced to the delight of the many patrons and Frank loved to watch me. Dancing and smiling I knew there would be no dancing for my guests.

"How many men do you think get to go home with one of the dancers?" Frank asked often as he gave me a hug.

My list coming to an end as the dancing began winding down, I knew what this dinner of mine would look like; my new tempo had created the menu. Satisfied with the result, it occurred to me that perhaps people in this area did not dance for the purpose of self-expression. To my knowledge there were no Gypsies here! I would have to ask Jennifer. The music ended and I decided to try another cassette. I was having fun! Soon enough my body responded to the movements of my hips. My arms, slithering, made their way somewhere above my head. I danced even if Frank could no longer see me. If Suzannah were here she would be telling me I was not a Gypsy. Mother would be appalled and Father would join me. If Maman ever saw me dancing it would have been when I was seven or eight, dancing with my blue shawl when I pretended to be an Arabian Princess. I laughed, as I remembered telling her during a moment not unlike this one, my name was Rashmina and my kingdom was Dreamland. Suzannah found the comment amusing and often after that would tell me to get out of Dreamland and get back to my lesson. Mother advised me I was not an Arabian. Maman never understood me, even when I was very young. She expected what was mysterious to me.

Two hours had passed, I danced and I had a menu and a grocery list to be purchased no later than Thursday. Just in case, one bottle of red wine would come from France. I felt vibrant and alive! The desire to escape life's many challenges brought by grief was gradually effacing itself. From my morose state of mind I had returned to my lighter side.

Conversations I once had with Suzannah were coming back to me in an undiluted form. For a long time I believed I paid little attention to what she said, I am finding how wrong I was. Mostly on the porch, I am allowing myself the freedom to explore feelings and memories buried but retained. This is all part of who I am. This process brought with it questions about what I may want to do to occupy my time in the near future. I would take care of Frank's papers but I wanted more. Ruminating memories was proving to be grounds filled with seeds to grow my existence in directions I could predict.

The possibility of new friendships brought succor to circumstances once believed impossible to surmount. I made a promise to myself to find many friends, even if I had to manufacture them out of thin air. As this probing of my psyche was going on, my mother's dishes were neatly put away. I examined each and nothing broke or chipped during their long voyage. On Saturday night I would celebrate in the dining room and would use the dishes. With this retrospective endeavor came the recognition of how I valued my mother; distant or aloof by nature, impossible to please, I missed her dearly. I could not help but wonder why, as a species we enjoyed tormenting one another. Tales long locked in my mind and waiting for the right moment to emerge were slowly making their appearance. Suzannah's anecdotes were brilliant and the wisdom I had not always acknowledged, I appreciated now. This woman was a powerhouse of information on thousands different subjects covering an era of life, not long in duration. She told me stories that had an impact on the lives of millions. I wish I had said something when her teaching sessions were underway. At the time, I did not know I was learning the content of Suzannah's vault of information. She was an authority on WWII, its stories and events but alas, my listening was unconscious. Now was the time to recall every word she spoke. I needed to unravel the qualities that made this woman so dear, so compassionate, so strong and yet, so enigmatic. She must have had secrets that no one would ever know. She had no friends but was not a bitter or angry person; she was what I call singular. She was stoic most of the time when she told her stories. She did not embellish or make excuses. She did not offer opinions. My own method of storytelling was exactly the opposite.

My surroundings were releasing what musical notes give to me sometimes, a value, an appreciation of things unseen, an undulation in time and a particular rhythm. This harbor could very well hold keys that would open many doors I locked. These rocking chairs had something to do with it, movement, maybe. I speculated that when I was very young Suzannah told me stories while rocking me. Those were special times when she substituted as kind of a nanny while my mother and father travelled. Aunt Erika was never asked although she resided in the house. Mother did not like her. She went out of her way to create disruption anytime I was alone with Aunt Erika. After my father died, she even burned letters belonging to Aunt Erika. Somehow my mother decided private letters between siblings were not important. That was the only time I ever saw my aunt in distressed, and angry. Mother found the letters when she was being impossible to be around. She went through all things private or otherwise, disposed of what she deemed unnecessary. She has sense enough not to go through Suzannah's things. My mother was not a secured person and because of it she was hurtful.

The old memories were becoming threadbare; I was discovering presents that needed to be unwrapped. Uneasy feelings were making way to ignored or long forgotten promises. Less than a mile away the waves moved in and out, as waves do. They were sending a signal I could almost touch but not yet grasp.

Almost four decades have passed in the blink of an eye. Yet this is another season in my life. As I look through the viewfinder, I see what appears to be a multi-scenic panorama. These days, when done with this type of self-indulgences, I no longer feel unbalanced. I have focus! Looking at the harbor, I am pointed toward the memories I have hidden from myself. The aperture is focused; the volatility of my mind is making room for something else. Right again, Suzanna! At one time I might have painted the canvas without thinking of what I was attempting to accomplish.

"Julienne, pay attention to everything around you. Put yourself in your surroundings and know every step you take has the potential to enhance or hurt you, and also others. Think, dear child, because with your thoughts and your actions you can change your world. Try to enhance your life and the life of those you encounter. Find good and virtuous reasons and follow the path. These are the things that make life worthwhile. Without patience you cannot get there. You will know when you have left Dreamland and entered reality."

These words resonated as I thought about that French class. I knew I would pay attention to each student and with care speak to him or her about learning and speaking French.

I have a clearer idea of what she alluded to. I continue to ask questions and they often remain unanswered. My problem is still patience, something I did not have as a youngster and continue to struggle with. I guess Suzannah knew that about me. Tenacity and persistence are the other traits I recognize she had. She acted with poise always. I realize mother had some of those qualities no matter how irrational she was with me. She lost patience with me, but tenacity and persistence never faltered.

I have noticed subtle changes in me; for one thing, I am less impulsive. The personalities of these two women could explain why Suzannah accepted without a fight mother's need that she should move away. She knew my mother had given it some thought and so her reasons were honored, not questioned. But why I still could not answer and did not like it.

The rocker, the porch and everything around me seemed to be a magic carpet to another world. The bourgeois existence I thought I was born to live had imprisoned my mind. I chose imaginary tale when reality was too difficult to harness. In this house everything was becoming real. My world was changing.

I missed Suzannah's essence. Alone and thinking about the assortment of paths I had taken and those she told me she took, I am left with colorful bands of events. Recollections kept safe in the vault between my ears represent the canvas she often talked about. One brush stroke at a time, I am making a masterpiece.

Suzannah would have been shocked or saddened by some of my blunders. My great adventures were not always of any consequence yet volumes could be written about them. Much like the blasted tattoo was a subject for conversation particularly when I disrobed for the pleasures of the flesh. When Suzannah told me about her tattoo she said nothing about the reaction mine would receive. Perhaps she did not know. As she said, hers had history while mine was a childish caprice. Looking at this event with honesty I found I had become more objective about my series of lustful encounters. Many things one regrets while enjoying the view from a porch.

I gazed upon the various wild flowers in the garden below the porch. The weather allowed them to play with my senses. I could see the similarities between Suzannah and my mother and why they were able to notice my questionable activities. This was the place where order would take a leap and establish itself. Living alone, I had the luxury of undisturbed time to ponder about and solidify the person that I was becoming. These days the ground is solid beneath my feet. New textures and colors are being added. The mirror of life has something distinguished to reflect. I am pleased.

Nadette

New discoveries about myself are making space for some stories to come crashing to the surface. None of the influential events in my life happened here. Yet, in this place with its differences, I found a channel I could explore.

The weather is different, the plants are not the same and no one was talking to me, and yet, I found myself attempting to sift through a maze left veiled deep inside. I am not always comfortable with the mind's wanderings. It is evident I must look at everything; I must solve riddles I did not recognize before. Had Frank not succumb to cancer, he could have helped me with the memories I have suppressed. He knew about the human psyche; he prodded mine often enough. When telling about American Literature, he had a way of superimposing and blending not only the psyche of the person he was talking about, but also mine. These were the qualities that made him a beloved professor. His students benefitted from him and I am awakening to what he knew was there. In the short time together, he got to know me well. I realize this but the reasons not yet clear to me.

My youth was lived with speed but today, in slower motion I can review everything. I left behind the things I could not confront and today I have the time to explain them to myself. If Frank or Suzannah were part of this dialogue, we would discuss, solve and rearrange the order of life itself. Frank and I had a good marriage; he was my friend, my lover my teacher; I feel the sadness associated with what I no longer have. They both talked about the same concepts. To them mankind was in need of community. With this in mind, do I create community around me, or do I join the community that already exists? Being different with an accent I may not be accepted. This would not be surprising, after all humanity goes to war over differences. People have to mentally organize their mind in ways to accept ideas different than what they are accustomed to. I struggle with these principles in relation to foods, dress or simple mode of living in a country other than the one I am familiar with.

Before he died Frank said, "We are lucky, Julienne. Not many married people are happy." I think it may be a matter of acceptance of whom we are mixed with love. I may never know."

At the time I felt the thought morbid, yet upon reflection, I realized few married people I knew were happy. Perhaps in America it was different. This man gave me the gift of his brilliant mind. Most people I have met since have never experienced such a gift. People do not really converse, they do not open themselves, and they do not say what they feel. Fear I guess keeps this from happening. We did the opposite and I think our happiness ultimately came from that space. No matter what the circumstances were, openness and candor were our partners.

A place to think, to be alone with my thoughts, and a place to weigh every issue that has ever occupied my mind, I am indeed lucky. My memories hold the key to what I am looking for. With a smile, I get up and embark on a walk toward the harbor, seven steps down and the long walk along the driveway. My hope is today the waves will reveal the secrets they hold.

My parents allowed Suzannah to teach me about the history and geography of Europe. She did not know much about America and neither do I.

"Lets begin with Poland because this is where my family was from. We will cross to the Mediterranean later. Much happened when I was young and much continues to happen."

Suzannah was a good teacher; the student however, had other interests. The last name on her mother's side was Weiss. She told me she was born Jewish and in Poland. Grandfather Cohen was a doctor. Her father was a doctor too. I am sure she told me much more but I had a bad habit of not paying attention when things did not interest me. I continue to hear her voice, "Pay attention, Julienne" she said, and now I know I did pay attention.

I feel guilty because of the times I allowed my mind to wander like knowing more about her family. The same was true with my mother but in her case, she gave lectures about the things I did not do right. My relation with the two most important women in my life was very different.

Frank insisted I could settle anything. He often told me the turmoil did not happen overnight and would take time to unravel, which is true. "Give yourself permission to explore who you are. You will love yourself more than I love you." Every time he said something like that, I think to reassure me, he would embrace me with his thinning arms.

Life has a way of being cruel. Walking the harbor would be different if he were next to me. He would talk to the people we passed. Frank knew how to engage people. I am still learning this art. All at once, I allowed myself to think again of getting a pet. If I did, I would at least have a walking companion.

Back home, I turned the radio on. The dial was set to a station playing a jazz piece, a type of music I was beginning to understand. Frank had a lot of classic jazz records and we often frequented places in and outside of Paris where American music was popular. Frank enjoyed jazz and the blues. The music changed and I realized I was beginning to understand how Suzannah might have felt. She had no family, only me. Looking around I saw neither family nor friends. Making friends was to be a matter of choice.

Of late, there was an agitation inside me. I cried for Suzannah yet could not muster the strength to approach the contents of the box she had left to me. The designs and the general look of it told me that she had spent time with the person who carved it. I was apprehensive about opening a box whose contents may have held answers to mysteries I was not yet ready to explore. Fear of things unknown was a close relative of mine. There was Suzannah's box and also a small one from Frank.

Based on its size, I suspect Frank may have left me a piece of jewelry. Not opened as of yet, this box is still wrapped with red paper. It was meant to be a Valentine day present but he could not give it to me. He had fallen asleep after the effort it took him to move to where his treasure was in our apartment. The time was never right to open the gift. Today I will celebrate Valentine day! It is not February.

I wanted to have a child with him. But, my way of thinking would have made an emotional wreck of this little person. As it is, I can take solace in the fact that the world is already over-populated and I did not ruin anyone's mind. I picked up by little box. This time I unwrapped my gift with care. I wanted to save the red paper with small hearts. Once I opened the box, a gold ring with two intertwined hearts awaited my finger.

Thinking about past conversations and events has two effects on me. I grow thirsty and I want to take a nap. Since I made a mental note not to nap in the afternoon, I have high tea with no crumpets. I walk down my seven steps, around the back of the house to a small garden with flowers. The mums are in bloom and I cut a few with scissors I have permanently left on a workbench. Walking back around and up the seven steps is my exercise for the day. For some reason, I do not use the back door. In the kitchen, I fill the kettle and start the electric stove, making a mental note a gas stove would be more appealing to me. The black tea is soon ready and I go to the dining room. I enjoy my tea in a new cup purchased in town. According to the sales lady, the storeowner whom I did not meet was from Poland. She had an accent but different than mine the young woman told me. I said I would return one day. Since Suzannah was also from Poland, this person could become my friend. On a mission to make friends, this encounter would become one of many. I took another sip of tea wishing I had a pastry.

Suzannah once told me her father was a doctor, but never said what kind. Could he have been a doctor who cared for the mind? Suzannah was always attentive to the soundness of mind and actions. She paid particular attention to mine. She had a thing about acting and reacting. She said she knew about both and no matter how difficult and uninspired her life may have been, she learned to act rather than react. She did say she reacted once and it changed her life. After a pause, she also said it was the best thing she ever did. I wonder now what disturbed this conversation because I do not know what she was referring to. I may never know. Still I reacted to her comments. During our tête-à-tête and sometimes rather lively discussions Suzannah would insist, "Difficult, yes, but not impossible. Julienne you can do these things when you have to." I had no idea what was so impossible and gave it no thought. Suzannah told me a story she had heard from a girl named Gerda. It was the story of the rape of Nadette, whose mother was a French Jewish woman who was taken to a camp. I can recall most of it and it went like this. The afternoon her mother was arrested, Nadette's life was spared because she had been waiting in line for bread tickets. When she returned home with no ticket and no bread she also had no mother. Her father had been in a prison in a town named Oswiecim. Not long ago I learned that Auschwitz was within this town. Suzannah never told me exactly when this horrific incident happened but I think she said it was around 1941 or 1942. I was not German or Jewish, so with my usual lack of interest, I did not ask questions or concern myself with people I did not know. The idea of waiting in line to get bread was something foreign to me. When I purchased my new batch of tea just two weeks ago, there was a line at the bakery and I decided not to wait. Now while sipping this cup of tea, I am reminded of Suzannah's story. She said war brought out the worst in people and the bread line was insignificant. I, on the other hand, could choose to wait or not.

"During times of war and also at other times, it appears many men have a need to exercise their power over others. They rape, they pillage, they burn, they destroy, and they take advantage of young and old alike. That is the panorama of life during a war." The importance of what she said did not seem important to me until now. I can think, I can question why human beings behave as they do.

"Julienne, humanity has many sides and offers surprises. At times, during moments of adversity, you will find men like your father who go out of their way to help others. You should respect and honor such people. In the course of your life, you will meet plenty of people who operate from opposite principles."

Suzannah liked and respected my father. I adored him! He always took the time to tell me how much he loved me. When I think of him, I still can see his tall silhouette, his black hair much like mine but cropped short. He wore colorful ties with white shirts. He was a handsome man.

The day she talked about the rape, she was not sitting in her favorite blue chair. Instead, she was at her very small dining table flanked by two overstuffed chairs, upholstered with a plaid fabric woven in Germany. She must have been looking through papers, for they covered the small table. I walked in, kissed her forehead and sat across from her while she told me about the various memories each piece of paper had inspired. That afternoon she allowed a steady flow of tears to cascade down on her face. I was surprised as Suzannah rarely allowed herself to cry. This was when she told me the story of Nadette who had been hiding all day after the rape. If I understood correctly, Nadette knocked on the door of a neighbor. It was very late and the mother, wife of the pastor, was already in bed. I gathered this incident had happened a very long time ago. Possibly the neighbor was Suzannah's neighbor as well. Some details continue to escape me or were vague to begin with. I did not ask enough questions because when events did not directly involve me I could not relate to them. This is something I am learning to change, and Suzannah would be proud of me for that. She was a good storyteller.

"No full moon to see by and the entire population of the village had gone inside because of the curfew. All was dark and silent except for occasional sirens sometimes followed by more explosions or fires. When the door opened the pastor's wife saw Nadette who was crying. Another girl came into the parlor; she had heard the crying. Nadette in rags, her face covered with dried blood and some teeth missing, clutching her clothes with both hands because they were torn to shreds. Nadette's entire body trembled. The other girl, Elga was her name, older than Nadette and also Jewish, had been hiding at the home of the pastor who had taken in five young women to save them from the Nazi soldiers who were always around. Nadette stared, expressionless for a long while. The silence said a lot and everyone knew nothing would ever again be right in her life. It took a while before Nadette began to tell her story."

According to Suzannah, this report came from Trudy and Elga, two girls she must have known but she did not tell me from where. Thinking about this story, I wish I could have been more caring and ask Suzannah for details. Though history has plenty such stories to explore, I know I am not the only one that did not care when told. Ashamed, in the comfort of my porch, I try to piece this account.

"Nadette found the back door to her parent's kitchen wide open. She felt something was wrong because even when the door was unlocked, it was kept closed. Nadette walked in to tell her mother there was no bread that day; she closed the door behind her. No one was in the kitchen and this was when she saw the broken glasses and dishes. She knew something bad had happened. She went into the dining room. That door was closed. She was petrified because she did not know what she would find and no one had ever closed the door before. She wanted to find her mother."

I could feel Suzannah's sadness; the tears were continuing to flow. Curving around her nose without reserve, resting a split second and down in front of her white blouse. Her right hand made the movement of turning a doorknob. Two SS soldiers jumped. "They were drinking and the smell of alcohol was intoxicating. The little dog, Fritz, came running toward Nadette. One of the two soldiers shot him while screaming obscenities both at her and the dog. 'Jews are not allowed to have dogs!'

Suzannah paused a while, I said nothing at all.

"Nadette bent down to hold her bleeding and dying dog. This was when she felt the hand of the shooter on her shoulder and neck. His hand felt like steel vice. She thought he would shoot her also but instead, he grabbed her from the shoulders and propped her against the dining room table. He held her down, shoving a towel in a mouth. The other soldier tore her clothes, mounted her like a dog and raped her. He slapped her repeatedly, dislodging the towel. It flew out of her mouth along with two of her teeth. They landed across the room and stopped by the fireplace. Blood flowed down her face and chest. One soldier found the scene amusing and laughed while she attempted to scream. Her rapist turned her around and repeated the assault. She saw the last drops of Fritz's blood in a puddle; he no longer moved. She said when the soldier was done with her; he turned her so she would face him. This time he threw some liquor in her face and threw her down. She landed on the floor next to her dog. She held Fritz but he could not comfort her, he was dead. The other man, strong and smelling worse than the first one, took her by the hair and propped her against the wall. Holding her head, he knocked it against the wall. She fainted and when she came to the soldier asked if she had enjoyed it. He got her on the table because her legs could not support her and like the other man he also raped her. They took her to the kitchen, opened the door and threw her outside. She fell like a bag of potatoes and as she did one of her attackers threw a coin on the ground as payment for her services. They called her a whore. "

I had never seen Suzannah cry like this before. I got up and brought her a glass of water. I gave her a hug and we held each other for a while. She told me how much she loved me. A moment later I asked her how old Nadette was when this happened.

The accuracy of my memories of this story surprised me as I wiped tears from my eyes.

"She was thirteen years old."

What happened to her Suzannah?

83

"She hung herself outside her home, under an apple tree. She was wearing the clothes given to her earlier by the pastor's wife. Her face was no longer bloody but that did not matter. Julienne, war of any kind is horrible people lose their reason for living there is no hope and suicide may seem like the only option. Jews usually do not take their own lives. We simply must not judge, we cannot judge but it is important to remember."

Suzannah told me she heard about this incident because Elga and Trudy came to live at the convent.

Rehashing elements of this story, I recognized the atrocities of war. How and why did some people lose their humanity? I cannot come up with answers. Would I have gone mad? Consumed by shame, with nothing to live for, no hope, no family or friend to run to gave Nadette the reasons she needed to commit suicide.

You Hold the Key

Suzannah's stories were often mysterious and yet they defined my psyche. My intention was to unravel the mysteries one after the other. Taking the time to do so would perhaps give me the means to find what I wanted know about this telegram in my mother's book. Aunt Erika often visited an orphanage, was there a relative I knew nothing about? I have no parents to enlighten me so one of these days I will return to France to find this orphanage and know Aunt Erika's secret.

It was time for something different and music sounded like the right medicine. Out of Frank's large collection of records one of Leonard Cohen attracted me. I played 'The Partisan." I felt this artist could have been close to Suzannah since her story and the lyrics were similar. Often words, places and now a song remind me of Suzannah.

"Julienne, your essential nature needs to be nurtured. If you do not take care of it, you will lose your soul and once it is gone, it will not come back. You, my dear, as the recipient and the carrier of this nature, must honor it. The people around you hold the colors that give meaning to your life but they do not hold the key to who you are."

The song told me about a partisan who died without surprise, of one who changed his name in order to survive, losing

85

wife and children. Suzannah and Frank had held the colors now on my canvas; they gave meaning to my life. The colors and the brushes responsible for whatever brilliance my canvas might contain came from them. She had this obsession that demanded that I find who I was. I remember once, while she was talking and I was half listening, I was eating a piece of blackberry pie she had taken out of the oven moments before. She was not too happy with me because I had cut into it while the pie was still hot. I can still smell the aroma but I cannot bake a decent pie. I wondered if the story she told me about eating berries and nothing else was true. Obviously, nothing she found in a forest could have tasted like her pie; the berries used came from her little garden behind the house. I had picked them the day before. While Maman planted flowers and very few vegetables, Suzannah's garden contained edible plants. "When you have had an empty stomach, this is the type of garden you want around." She said to me.

She spent a great deal of time in this garden; every fruit, every leafy vegetable and root was always delicious. I could not help but laugh when Suzannah sang to her plants. I caught myself talking to the plants in my garden. I do not sing to them, not yet!

"Much like the flowers you talked about when you went to the botanical garden, you need to remember to honor the essential nature of your own flower garden, the one inside you." Through metaphors Suzannah explained life to me. Her words were fluid and did not slide through my fingers. I now I savor what she meant.

"You need to know who you are and what makes you tick, Julienne! With effort will you ever be able to make your world one with fewer tears. A world you feel comfortable in."

When I was young and cried and felt sorry for myself, usually because a boy did not like me, Suzannah made no secret of her disapproval of this reprehensible behavior. She had no tolerance for such imbecilities, she said. Today when I cry, I know the reason why and I am grateful for the insights. Suzannah would be happy to discovery a degree of gratitude has replaced the prior behavior.

I can see her with her navy blue skirt and one of her white long-sleeve blouses. She did not cross her legs the way I do. She had two reasons, one was something about circulation and the other was a way women sat to expose their thighs. She went on and on to enforce her idea and it took me quite a while to understand what her point was. Now, when I sit I do not cross my legs. I prefer to keep my feet on the ground, on terra firma, Frank commented with smiles.

I got up and walked to my bedroom, still day dreaming I realized how much I liked the pillows on the bed. They are a dim representation of the ones Suzannah had on her chairs. Two throw pillows with a peacock in the center of each. She called the cloth a toile and she made the pillows herself. Shades of blue appealed to Suzannah and peacocks held a special meaning for her. There must be something about these birds but whatever it is still eludes me but I like them. Aunt Erika told me she gave the toile to Suzannah but I thought my father did when he returned from a trip to India. The toile was re-embroidered with threads of gold and silver. Suzannah's entry door had been painted blue to blend with her new pillows and chairs. These were the items you first saw when you entered her little house. My front door is now almost the same shade of blue. There was a time when I would have preferred a red door. To that Suzannah would have said red carried too much blood for her taste while the blue created an atmosphere of serenity for her and it does so for me too.

Mysteries were all around her and I loved it. Everything had a reason; this is something I am beginning to encounter in my own life. Suzannah went out of her way to keep me guessing and I am still guessing.

Amazing how deeply her spirit has settled inside my soul. I think Maman felt this bond between us and did not care for it. Perhaps the time spent with Suzannah was responsible. We played together, she talked a lot, and sometimes I listened.

"You determine your final identity, observing, perceiving what touches you are only partially responsible; they are tools available for your use. The choices you make determine how well you chose. Try to make choices that will bring you no shame or bring others pain. Those are hard to live with. In the end, how you react is what molds you. You alone are accountable for who you are and what you do. Only you, remember this, Julienne. There is nothing mysterious here. I feel at this time it is something you know nothing about. Learn to wait a moment, stop and evaluate your actions. Life is a series of lessons we learn from. What you think, how you distinguish everything around you will determine not only who you are to yourself but also how others will judge you. Those are the things that will make you a better human being. Examine your mother's garden. Watch the flowers. They are nurtured, watered and nourished, and because of all this care, they open fully and offer those looking at them the brilliance of their nature. It all takes work, my dear. You are like one of the flowers being nurtured, watered and nourished. Like one of the very beautiful flowers, you too have a limited time use it wisely. That is how it is. How you react is what's important and believe me, your reactions, provided they are not out of some insane whim or illusion, will be the only indicator you can trust to carry you to destination. You hold the key Julienne."

These conversations had elements of vagueness or they irritated me. Only now I can decipher what Suzannah was saying to me. The saddest part is that I did not apply many of her principles to my personal life. At least these days, I am aware of the people who were in my life and I can appreciate the gifts they left me with. Who I am today is because of them. So often she urged me to be patient, to observe, and pay attention. The complete picture is coming into view. I am finding life is a process demanding a great deal of patience.

"If you can do this, you will know a type of freedom many never find. This takes practice but I think you have the tenacity and the preparedness for it. You have to want it more than life itself. Believe me, I know what I am talking about. It is what resides between your ears, the stuff of life no one can touch. Dear girl, the freedom I am talking about resides inside you, no matter what the conditions."

I got it! Suzannah was free long ago and at peace with the choices she made. Me, with my dinner parties, travel and friends, I am only touching the surface. Like Suzannah, Frank had this inner freedom I know not enough about. Neither Suzannah nor Frank are in my life now, yet they continue to be the water I swim in, the wind that blows beneath my wings, and the deep love they offered as a gift will carry me to my destination. I miss the support they gave to me. The porch and the peripheral escape enable me to revisit the past to find the right road. Suddenly, I have a better sense of what freedom is and the idea came when I was not looking. Reaching this elusive state of mind, Frank and Suzannah talked about, is an act of will. The mere idea of it is simply not sufficient. I lived the first part of my life without grasping this basic concept, I also know I am not alone with my discoveries. Suzannah tried hard to teach me and had the idea taken hold years ago, many things would have been different. The waters have changed their course and I can either change with them or stay on shore. Walking forward on a road I do not know seems the only logical path.

This porch, the breeze, the view, the stillness, and for certain the rocking chairs are all the instruments present to assist me. A thought passes through in a flash. I wish I could tell them. I am happy where I am. The preparedness Suzannah talked about is behind a door I can finally open. Mother would be pleased if she knew. Perhaps I would receive an accolade from her. I smile knowing Maman knew very little about accolade.

"Remember to shield yourself and those you love from great pain. You will encounter continual challenges. Life seems to be one struggle after the other. Happiness and contentment are there to be found. You will meet people who manipulate you and others who nurture you. Mankind seems to work in this manner and it will be up to you to ascertain the differences. First my dear, you must know yourself. The traps are wide and deep and sometimes because of our personal perceptions, we imprison ourselves or we render others responsible for the things we do. Julienne, once we get inside the prison, it is not easy to get out. We do things we would not do under normal circumstances. Fear has a way of altering things and people too. Primal instincts kick in. We miserably lose track of who we are. The only person you need to nurture is you. You control nothing else. Remember the story I told you about Nadette? She did not know that with patience, perseverance, she could have found the tools to conquer the shame she harbored. I do not even know if this is correct. What those men did to her she could never forget. I do not mean to imply that one must forget. One needs to continue on. I told you many times that you control only you. These things will become clear to you as you get older."

She told me these things and now my rocking chair tells me when we are hurt, the pain lessens with time but the memories remain. It is peculiar how that works.

"It seems that war gives license to be vile and evil usually in the name of country, freedom, purity of race, or religion. I think fear is also a motivator in war. I find the whole of humanity using excuses to justify despicable behavior. Julienne, sometimes I feel my shame is to be part of the human race. But I must go on. I told you that many times it is up to each of us to improve who we are and how we behave. When you are about to do something think about what effect it will have. Think of those you will hurt; think of how you will hurt yourself. Remember, Meine Liebe, you hold the key. Take the time to examine issues as they are but not how you would like them to be. Be responsible for what you do. No one but you is ever responsible. As you grow older, learn to weigh your actions and your options. Be honest with yourself and others too. If I have one wish for you it is for you to become a balanced adult. Of course, we both know that adulthood for you is a simply matter of the next moment."

I was seventeen years old and not a child when we had this conversation. Suzannah treated me as a precious piece of silver, always removing some invisible tarnish.

"What you hold onto with your mind and your heart and what you let go off will tell the tale. Think about these things, Julienne. It is of course, easier to blame others. Try not to run your life this way. Learn to be comfortable in your own skin. Be a person you can respect. No facsimile can ever be as satisfying."

Each word of this conversation kept playing in my head like a phonograph record that was stuck. It was not on my tattoo day but it was a perfectly clear sunny day years before my twenty-first birthday. These conversations were sometimes unnerving yet they deeply impacted and influenced my life. I did not think about them the night before that birthday when twenty-one meant freedom to me.

The Honey

I feel her essence near me, a hint of her scent tickles me sometimes, and most of all in my mind I see her smiling at me. The same feeling encircles me when I think of Frank. This happens when I am inexplicably at peace with myself. The presence of my Mother or Father in my life has taken a different space yet I miss them both but neither invades my reveries. I suppose it is because each person experiences love differently. I have no one to ask so I will accept the fact that my mother and my father demonstrated their love differently. The teachers around me are now gone and lessons come from various other sources. I am noticing the world with acumen, imagery and nuances. The impressions arrive to me like an abstract painting might appear. It is a matter of seeing — and deciphering, a matter of understanding the core. The blank canvas Suzannah thought I was is almost completely filled. Each brush stroke is visible. The canvas is the sum total of all who held a brush to it. Where I am to go from the point of reference remains to be seen and continues to be a work in progress. Suzannah often implied I did not know who I was. Somehow, I managed to open doors I locked long ago. A flood came in carrying with it the light I needed. The time to escape was at an end. Mistakes I made and their price could have been avoided but they were not. Many people were hurt, including me because I thought only of myself.

My father said often that life was to be lived, I wonder how many mistakes he made? Suzannah told me when the time was right I would find all the answers to my questions. Almost forty now, I am happy with the person I have become and still I do not have all the answers.

I see her smile as she said inside my head was like a beehive. "Bzzz, bzzz. It takes time for the honey to be produced!" Suzannah was funny, and sometimes I wonder if she ever considered how long it would take for me to taste the honey she talked about.

The fog on this day was dense. I could barely see the gate at the end of my long driveway. But then, someone opened it. The small truck made it in and stopped by the stairs. It was James man jack-of-all trades who could repair anything. Today he carried a special sprayer. After the proper but distant greetings, he explained what he intended to do. With chemicals he was going to exterminate the bugs in my garden. I felt a sudden jolt. The word "exterminate" resurrected a story I decided to tell him after informing him there would be no extermination on this property.

"James, please allow me to tell you why I do not want chemicals to exterminate anything on this property. We will have to come up with something else, like learning to live with the bugs. The vermin, as you called them, are not hurting me or destroying anything around me. So they eat some of the fruits. But so do I. He smiled when I said that. Anyway, let me share my story with you.

96

"I was about eight or so when I saw a bug in my mother's garden. I ran to her, getting my shoes dirty on the wet and muddy dirt, I told her about a horrible bug I had just seen. Not a butterfly or one of the abundant ladybugs that were always around. This intruder was larger than any bugs I had seen before. I did not know its name and it did not matter. It scared me because it had multiple legs, was green and crawled in a way that caused me to run. I suggested that an exterminator be called to take care of all the bugs in the garden. A few days before, I had learned words like *eradicate* and *exterminate,* the perfect words to justify what I had in mind. My mother acknowledged my distress but did not do anything about it. I did what I always did, I ran to see Susannah. By the way, she lived in a little guesthouse behind our house. I never told you about her but I told Jennifer about her. Anyway, I told Suzannah about this bug and suggested once again that an exterminator should come right away and eradicate the undesirables. The solution, I said to her, was to have them forcibly gone. She turned to get a better view of my face. She did that a lot."

Now let me tell you what she said to me. She was long winded but I will be as short as I can.

"Julienne, do you know the meaning of the words you use exterminate, eradicate, those are strong words child?"

"The bugs needed to be exterminated so none would survive!" I answered. With the look again and taking my hand, she walked me outside to the cement bench painted white not far from the pond. We had a very beautiful fishpond in our yard; something I may want to duplicate here. Anyway, It was a beautiful day; the flowers were all in bloom. When I looked toward her blue door I noticed she had two new pots. They were large and mustard yellow. They were filled with lavender. I had not noticed them when I burst in to tell her about the bug and the impending extermination."

James looked at me not knowing what to say, my digressions were perhaps confusing him.

"For a while she said nothing at all, then I noticed her eyes. They looked dark but not menacing. Her face appeared different as she held both my hands. I noticed that hers were trembling a little. In a soft voice, almost inaudible she said, 'Not too long ago, someone else tried extermination; but this time there were people involved. Millions of people died but this systematic process known as The Final Solution did not exterminate all Jews. Remember that, Julienne, the next time you have thoughts of extermination."

"Since that day, I have developed an aversion toward chemical extermination. The bugs were here a long time before I ever set foot on this property."

"Mrs. Fairchild, I understand where you're coming from I didn't know you were Jewish, I should have chosen different words."

It had not been my intention to embarrass James, but he was, I could tell, he was beet red.

"No, I am not Jewish, but the lady I told you about was. She experienced a lot of atrocities and now I finally understand what all of it means. No need ever to exterminate although, at times, we may feel the urge."

James smiled and picking up his five-gallon tank of chemical his apparatus with a pump attached to its head; he walked back to his truck. My bugs were safe for the moment. I decided to make a point to find natural predators. Talking to James about extermination caused me to think back many years.

"Suzannah, why did they want to kill Jews? Were they not people just like us?"

Suzannah smiled at me as she stroked my long curls. "Well, sweet child, I do not know the reasons why people do what they do. Anyone can find a good reason for the bad things they do. It seems to be the way of the human race. I have a hard enough time with what I do every day, what I did, and also the things I agreed to do many years ago. I think we can all explain to others or justify to ourselves anything even if we have to lie to ourselves or to others to do so. When you get older you will see that ethics is often a missing element in character. In the meanwhile, Julienne, try to come up with solutions better than extermination."

The significance of this conversation eluded me when I was young but today it is presenting me with new challenges. The riddles of my youths are coming home to roost. Now, I must find the more acceptable solution in order to keep the bugs out of my garden.

Uncharted Reflections

While growing up I used to think Suzannah was a peculiar person who could not understand me because she was too old-fashion or too foreign. These days we could talk about understanding. A case in point was the day she saw my tattoo; this was the time of my life when I believed the world revolved around me. I would gladly subject myself to her scrutiny and discuss with her why I voluntarily had myself branded. If we had such a conversation now, I would not linger on my tattoo but on hers. The tattoo that became an integral part of the stories she told me. I would ask her if she felt violated or was it a mixture of terror, anger and fear? I would ask if she was ashamed of it? I would ask her how she felt about it today? Most of all I would also ask her if she forgave the person who branded her? I remember feeling shame when Frank first saw my tattoo. I think any discussion about tattoos, hers or mine, would prove to be insightful. I am sure such a conversation would provoke both tears and laughter because a warped sense of humor was alive in the people I loved. She would help me recognize the theatrics of my youth and Frank would contribute some playfulness to the dialogue. He used this tool often when conversations needed to be diffused. I miss the gatherings we had in our apartment where international politics, music and various arts were the topics of discussion. Some of his students were in attendance to participate in great debates. I even miss some of them. Frank was eloquent; his mind was like quicksilver; he mastered the French language far better than the average person. As this flood of recollection came back to me, I knew I was the one with a problem. The red arrow on my ass is a reminder of idiocy when I was twenty-one. I wish I could still see the broad smile on Frank's face. He had a way of turning his head just far enough for me to kiss his cheeks. He liked a kiss on each cheek, yet he was not French. I missed the sensation I felt during those precious and tender moments. There is so much I did not tell those I loved. I did not think it necessary to let them know how important they were in my life. I never had time to examine, perceive and appreciate the little things. No longer can I experience the pat on the head or Suzannah's hand playing with my curls. Frank did the same but he aroused me differently.

The constant assaults from my mind have shifted, making room for instant probing when I meet new people. I want to know him or her. I want to know what makes them tick and I am not afraid to allow them to know whom I am. The time for the superficial vagabond is over. Had I practiced this need for knowing when Susannah was talking I would not be wondering about the people in her stories. I would know, and ask her to clarify what I did not understand. I would know if she felt anger or terror.

I did not give up when Frank's prognosis came back without a glimmer of hope; I lived for what we had and what we were sharing. He talked to me as much as he could about this house, the one he would never see and yet urged me to live in for him. He said there was something about the water that called him. I am living for both of us now and, in the process, I am beginning to know myself better. Did Frank know this would happen? Based on the stories I heard from Suzannah, I have a few questions for myself: How would I have felt? How would I have behaved? Would I be courageous? How strong would my convictions be? I think of the story she told me about Nadette, undoubtedly commonplace during a war. I have no idea how I would have reacted. Perhaps it is impossible to speculate about such things. How often was a young girl raped because a soldier had a need to exercise his sense of power? He may have been frightened himself. He may have had some bestial needs. I wonder what great psychiatrists think about these things. Are the questions and answers the same today since rape is not limited to war? I fail to find satisfactory answers for the human predicament. The ordeal faced by those who did not leave home soon enough remains with me. Will I ever understand the ravages of war? Will my mind ever be able to sort these things out? I, who was not directly affected, inquire about it. I know both Suzannah and Frank would have given me the words to make acceptance easier. Alas, this is something I will have to resolve on my own.

I think of conversations I heard about the Jewish predicaments, I think of those who helped them and those who did not. Suzannah was of the opinion that people did what they thought they had to. She brought simplicity to acceptance and human behavior to a simple primal need for survival. She said perhaps we were born with a seed to survive. She told me often enough it was that instinct to survive and the dreams of a clearer, brighter future that allowed many to hang on. She also said many were saved because they relinquished their wealth to others. Not smiling she also told me about greed. For the moment I was questioning if a soldier forgot that he raped or that he killed because a yellow star. Did he not see the person behind the star? Years later, how does that feel? Can an entire life be lived pretending to be a citizen with moral values? Is there a struggle to reconcile values not understood at the time? To this I think both of my loves would say, "People often do not think of the consequences brought on by their actions." I observe humanity, including me, and realize too often we still do not think of consequences.

Suzannah told me she believed a tormentor did not think much about the tormented. In order to hurt people they probably had been dehumanized, at least in their minds. Could this possible be? We would have endless debates if the three of us could sit and talk. I observe my immediate surroundings, filled with lush vegetation, birds, and even a deer or two and I feel very much alone and conflicted. I have not met people to expose to my debates to. Nature around me has little or no arguments except for the caterpillars eating leaves I would prefer to find untouched. Since caterpillars become butterflies I will await the birth of colorful butterflies. They too are in transitions. I wonder what I will become.

My mind feels as if it were floating again and having nothing better to do, I allow it to continue to wander along uncharted terrains. One day soon I will open the beautiful box Suzannah left me before she died. I do not feel ready yet. I find myself afraid to know its content. Why, I ask myself.

"If we manage not to be afraid of final outcomes, we can find freedom." Suzannah must have struggled with both and found a solution to the dilemma I face every day. I think she had no fear and, as a result, she found the inner freedom she spoke of. From her stories I know she was well acquainted with fear and also freedom or the lack of it. The difference between us is she conquered her fears and I am still working on mine.

My intention is to stay on track and I will find clarity, a degree of acceptance, and I will visit the mental freedom this woman so clearly displayed.

Years of listening to Suzannah and Frank have helped me to attain some depth of character. I must admit, at least to myself, I am far from my goal.

According to Suzannah fear is detrimental to evolution because it is paralyzing. Looking back at my life, I know I spent years in utter immobility. I became aware of this after Suzannah left the guesthouse. I was left with a damaged soul; something inside me was broken. I was paralyzed with something out of balance and nameless. No matter how much I searched my psyche the connection we had remained mysterious. The love for Frank and the loss of this man in my life left me with a void and yet also enriched. I felt a constant longing for Suzannah.

Like a tornado, my mind waltzed toward another time. I saw it again, Suzannah rolling down her sleeve as if to punctuate with a period the end of our conversation about tattoos. Her blouse had no more starch than any other day; perhaps, she had a special secret for combining the perfect blend between starch and cloth. The white linen, almost blue against the cream colored wall behind her gave her eye color a purplish tint. They got that way sometimes. The change in her eyes color was an indication that something more penetrating was about to happen. There was a great deal of unspoken dialogue between us. I miss that, too.

A simple glance and this woman could change the course of what I was doing or thinking. Maman could do it too; I could bend the will of Suzannah but never my mother's. Neither of them was with me when I got my tattoo. Perhaps a look would have been enough to change this portion of my life. Maybe the new friends would not have had such a grip on me. Alone with my rocker and sipping last year's chamomile tea, I have come to the conclusion Suzannah and my mother were right at least ninety percent of the time. I think today if they were here, together on this porch, we could have talked about the things we evaded. Perhaps with brutal honesty I would have asked Maman why Suzannah had to depart. I trust the two women understood each other because they were very much alike. I was missing something that only they could clarify.

Maman would have liked this part of the world. The lush vegetation alone would have attracted her. I wonder what type of flower garden she would plant here. Something inside felt tender as I thought of my mother's garden, its scents and what it represented in her life and mine too.

Suzannah, on the other hand, would walk the beach with me. She would use this method to punctuate conversations and tell me new stories. She would continue to explore the subjects left open for debate. Going deeply into my psyche was something she did well.

The Lunar Calendar

The leaves were changing color; the entire New England area was displaying shades of orange, amber and rust mixed with purples and browns. Something magnificent was happening. I was participating in a dance with nature. My colorful path to the house had lost its green luster, favoring shades of autumn. Ground covers were still green along with the variety of pine trees. They seemed to have changed to a deeper shade of green. All was new to me because in the South of France the seasons did not go through such drastic changes. Every morning when I walked outside the performance was magical, the air was crisper, and something delightful was happening. Perhaps the coolness was awakening me to a new day. Often when I went out I wore the shawl Frank had given me. When I received it I did not know its colors would be duplicated all around me. That night under a full moon and cold winds I thought of yet another time.

I was about sixteen when Suzannah told me about the Lunar Calendar. It was a brisk fall day, a rare occasion around the Mediterranean coast. She was fashioning a beautiful group of candles made with blue beeswax sheets. I never knew where she got anything. As far as I knew she never went out and she did not travel. Yet all around her were fascinating things for me to explore and learn about. I relished going through her collections and

109

assortments of beads and stones and other treasures. For my sixteenth birthday, she made me a pair of earrings; I wore them when Frank and I were married. She had tiny pearls in a coiled cluster, the whole thing no larger than a small coin. I would have preferred long earrings with dangling pearls. She knew this and when I opened my gift she reminded me of my age. Suzannah had fastidious unshakable ideas about this sort of thing and so did my mother.

This morning when I put them on, I had to laugh. Was I hoping for another sixteenth birthday? Mother and Suzannah were in agreement when it came to what I could and could not do at any given age. "Everything in its own time" Suzannah would say again and again. "Not appropriate" Maman said often as she dismissed me. As for the pearls Suzannah may have known my mother was giving me a pearl necklace on my sixteenth birthday. In any case Maman approved of the earrings. It was soon afterwards I passed my Baccalaureate exams. The teachers had done a good job and I hoped for a substantial reward. A car was my expectation, but for such extravagance, I had to wait. Achievement with schoolwork was expected of me, not rewarded with gifts. I could not change the mind of my parents about this. Something else I did not understand about parents. For a very long time I felt no one in my family understood my needs. I often thought none of them had ever been young. I had great hopes that someone would surprise me with a car. I could not let go of my expectations. Suzannah told me hope was a good thing to have. She said it kept things going and again I had no idea what she was talking about. She insisted I needed to exercise patience. She too did not understand me or the fact that I needed a car.

Nearly a month had gone by since the candle making experience and the disappointment of not receiving a car. One early December day when I opened the blue door, I found her hard at work making the most unusual candleholder. I helped her with candle making it was not difficult but for this intricate work; one needed to be a silversmith and a wood carver. I was neither. Suzannah never told me she could do these things and I still have no idea where she learned these arts. Out of her hands and creative fingers wood pieces and silver wires were being intertwined to hold the eight individual candles she had made. The one I made was also awaiting its place on center stage. My candle reminded me of a gargoyle with an elongated head. Making candles was not one of my talents. She told me one candle was the assistant; my candle was this special helper. The poor thing could not be anything else. It lacked beauty but Suzannah thought it was good-looking. She was kind always. She had mysteries to share when we were together. She told me we could light the candles together, one every night, just before darkness. She said it was a tradition and this year it was important because the new creation held meaning for me. I had made the helper. As she was telling me, she took a moment to show me how to twist the silver wire around pieces of wood. It came out like a bird's nest not exactly the expected work of art I had in mind. My creation was different from the ones she so delicately created. Beauty accompanied by a beast, I told her, but to her my creation was perfect. She did not know the prayers that went along with lighting the candles. Being part of her candle and candelabra making was enough for me.

"At home, no one talked about prayers, we were not religious and for a long time I lived in a Catholic convent."

In the missal my aunt had given to me years before, I did not find anything about such candle arrangements, kosher or otherwise. Perhaps I did not look far enough or in the right places. My interest about the lighting of a candle on any particular night was confined to Suzannah's kitchen. Something sweet and delicious each night to go with the celebration was quite enough for me. It took her days of hard work, to finish her Menorah as she called it. When she was satisfied with it, the candles were placed where they belonged.

When I went to visit her one evening, she handed me a box of matches and asked me to light the helper. She must have pressed the wax with something and created an intricate design around each candle. Where there was nothing before, a vine of wax grew. I wondered how she did it but did not ask. When I entered her small living room she suggested I join her for a slice of pie, adding that she had a story to tell me. I still have this Menorah; I keep it in my library and sometimes in my bedroom.

"The Traboules in Lyon saved many, including me. They were built by the Romans around the 4th century and were used by people transporting from silk to water and during the time of the Holocaust they became a route many took to safely. We entered them very late one night. We were five girls and one boy, guided by an old man. You have no idea how often I moved from one place to the next; this was yet another such journey. We walked up and down stairs and hallways. The guides kept changing. They were all French and most of them were old. We did not know who was guiding us or where we would end up. We could no longer experience fear; a sort of resignation had taken over. War has a way of bending your will and at some point you simply exist. Julienne, did I ever tell you about the Traboules? At times we were hauled through doorways we did not even see. No one told us where or what we would find. The old man and the woman who rescued us were French and we spoke German. Many people in France, at least where I was, had joined the Resistance. Others did not. Your father was part of the Resistance and its underground movement. We walked miles, rode trucks covered with hay. This was particularly dangerous because the hay was to be delivered to the German cavalry. But in order to make haste great risks were taken. There were not many horses left, they had been slaughtered for food. Sometimes people were captured and immediately sent to work or death camps. Three of the girls with our group had managed to escape while on a transport train to a death camp. Many camps were discovered after the war and few people came out of them. Gabriela, the older of the escapees told me there was a gap in the cattle car where they were crammed like sardines. They were small girls and could slip through the gap, they knew they would die and with nothing to hope for, they jumped, one after the other. The train slowed down and five girls jumped. Two were shot but Abira, Gabriela and Miriam lived to tell their stories as we walked that night toward a place we did not know. We all spoke German. We were nowhere near home and speaking our own language felt good. Simple expressions of feelings, a word, a smile and an occasional laugh gave something tangible to hang onto. They did not know if the two wounded girls were still alive, but they knew they had to run as far as they could in order to spare their own lives. We all prayed they were alive and rescued. Miracles did happen, you know! Praying was difficult because most of us had lost so many friends and relatives we did not have much faith left. Most of the French people we met in the Traboules were very helpful, some were not. I learned not to judge, no matter what people did because, when there is war, it seems to me the senses vacate the heart and mind and give way to primal survival. Gabriela said many of her old neighbors turned people in, sometimes for bread or potatoes. War is horrible, always! When one's very survival is at stake, one does what one must. I think this is a law of survival. We are creatures capable of so much that we can be proud of. Yet we are capable of extreme cruelty. I hope as you grow into womanhood, you will not have to reflect upon things that caused you shame or pain. Most of all make all attempts to hurt no one. I also hope you do not experience cruelty as a condition of war. Gabriela told of one of her neighbors who pointed her family out to some SS soldiers. This woman received two loaves of bread. She had six children and one was very sick, her husband was dead. Mrs. Schmidt did what she needed to do. You know, Julienne, I can imagine how that woman felt. She had to choose between betraying her Jewish neighbor and friend, and keeping her children alive. People should not have to make such choices. War is a horror! It does not matter which side you are on the soul becomes tainted if not destroyed."

We paused often when Suzannah told me her stories.

"I do not remember how long we walked, sometimes in complete silence and darkness. At times we found ourselves laughing at the most ridiculous things. We walked an eternity, in and out of tunnels and doorways, surrounded by noxious odors. At times I think we were lost. We climbed steps and walked narrow hallways sometimes I know we were underground. It was too dark to see past the shoulder of the person in front of us. In some areas, as if a magician had preceded us, we would find a basket with bread and sometimes water. Those were the times when faith was restored, yet the more we walked the more everything looked the same. Looming dark shadows broke the monotony and frightened us at times. Late at night an older and very frail gentlemen, one of

115

our guides, knocked on a large door several meters high. I could tell the wood was incredibly old. From the outside we heard latches being released and once the door was open we could see a great hall and found ourselves in another place that was foreign to us. It was a convent and we were all Jews. Instinctively, we understood once more we had been spared rape, starvation or a gas chamber. The walls was painted white and looked spotless. There were pictures of saints and crucifixes between doors that were not open. The lady who escorted us told us the names of saints as we passed them. She was dressed in a long navy blue garment with something like a bib in the front and wore something on her head like nothing I had ever seen. She told us her name was Sister Anne. We learned later on she was wearing the standard nun's habit.

"We were escorted to a large room with benches all around forming rows with spaces to walk down a center aisle. Each of us was given a package and next we were taken down another hall. It felt like decades since I had had a real bath. There were tubs five per row, filled with warm water and separated by a curtain. Only after our heads were checked for lice, (we had none), were we allowed to get to a tub. The boy with us had gone with a man dressed in a brown long robe. My hair had grown a lot but the three girls had almost no hair. Theirs had been shaved and perhaps because they were so undernourished their hair had not grown much. Our new clothes were uniforms much like the nuns wore dark blue almost black with a patch of white on the chest. It felt strange to be wearing these garments. Only our faces and the tips of our fingers showed. We did not complain because we knew how lucky we were. We paraded proudly, wearing our new clean clothes. There were no mirrors so we told one another how wonderful we looked. Soon enough we were taken to another hallway and it opened into a dining room. I do not know what time it was, late in the evening probably, as we sat down around a long table. Someone called Mother Superior came in and greeted us. A few seconds later, the man in a dark robe entered the room. He was introduced to us as Father John Francis. With his right hand he made a sign in the air while saying something in Latin. The nuns made the same sign on their chest. Look, Julienne, it is the sign of the cross, with the right hand, up to the forehead, down the middle of the chest, then the shoulders, forming a cross. I think it was a remembrance for Catholics. No, no you have it wrong. Try again it is easy. We also learned the words in French, *Au nom du père, et du fils,* would you believe it, I do not remember the rest. The sign of the cross is something all Catholics do. There! You did it! Bravo! You should know that, you are a Catholic. In that dining room we were given the largest bowl of soup I had seen in a long time. Lots of vegetables floated in the pinkish thick broth. Each bowl contained at least three pieces of meat. I can still taste it and did not know I was so hungry."

When Suzannah told me a story, she often stopped at the halfway point, leaving me in suspense.

Suzannah reported to me about a Gypsy gathering that did not take place because so many had been killed or sent away. It was understood that the Germans were carrying out their bizarre cleansing of the human race while they were in France and everywhere else they were.

"A large quantity of French men and women helped the Germans and this made life difficult in the convent. If a girl looked too Jewish, she had to be kept out of sight for safety's sake. In the attic, most of the time we did not talk about such things; fear and shame were undoubtedly the reasons. Among the people, those who helped were afraid to be found. Those who did not were also afraid because of their decisions. War brings survival instinct to the forefront, and fear seems to dominate, it was difficult to know what motivated people, at least during WWII."

Many conversations we had are still with me. Suzannah had a hard life and yet, she did not display anger toward anyone.

"People were shot, children of all ages were often left to their own devices in woods, in town, etc. Labor camps were the ultimate fate for the stronger ones and the gas chambers for most. I heard of a particular doctor who did terrible experiments with people. (He was called The Angel of Death,) I could not decide if it was worse to be worked to death or to go directly to the ovens. It was late in the war when I accepted the reality of the gas chambers. Before that, I could not make myself believe what I was hearing. To have a normal life one day was my hope for survival. The hardest

118

thing during this time was not to despair; this was hard to overcome since fear was a constant companion. The people experiencing hopelessness did not survive well, not even when they were relatively safe. Self-preservation became a way of life. I was very young when I heard my mother's screams and also the shots. I was paralyzed with fear and did not run to help her. I did what I was told and now I live with that knowledge every day. I could not have helped her, yet I feel guilty because I did not try. The emotional self and the rational one are not one and the same. My mother gave up her life because she felt it was the way to keep us alive. With the help of sister Bernadette's kind talks I came to accept what I could not change. I did the best I could to preserve my life. I do not know what ever happened to Sister Bernadette; she was my life saver."

Suzannah talked about events not relating to me personally and I felt her pain. Often unable to deal with it, I left her. If only I could turn back the clock, I would have shown her some compassion.

All along I had been affected by the stories she told. The telephone rang, and with the sound my reveries ended.

Monique

The telephone rang, something rare here, I knew few people. This time, however, an offer to receive a daily paper was well received. The idea of learning about the area and perhaps finding things to participate in was like a breath of fresh air.

It was on a gloomy afternoon that Suzannah told me about a girl who came to the convent. Her parents owned a large inn in a town on the border of France and Germany. The place was secluded with woods all around and the SS officers liked that. The inn became a place where they would rest and entertain their women friends.

"Monique was a little bit German and a little bit French. Her father was in France, he met her mother and they were married soon after. Meister Klaus was born just across the border in where Monique and her parents went often to visit family. Monique did not talk very much about her parents. At the convent we felt something odd about her. During the war her mother was sympathetic to the Resistance and her father's allegiance was to the Fatherland. Suzannah surmised tension existed in Monique's home, and perhaps this is why she did not talk about her parents. If the story told was true, Monique was a precocious thirteen-year old, and had a dangerous encounter with one of the officers. Her parents arranged for her to travel to Lyon where her uncle had a home and a business. Monique hated the idea; she felt abandoned by her parents and angry because the officer she befriended and said she was in love with did not come to her rescue. She was a confused, angry young girl. Whatever the incident, it required immediate action by her family. There may have been more to it, something was not convincing. She talked about wishing and being permitted additional time with the tall officer. She indicated they were in love. This popular and convenient inn was within meters from a railway station, the route to a camp, but she did not know which one, and she did not particularly care. Her officer Hans she called him, had a special compartment and that was all she cared about. At the inn soldiers arrived in cars, motorcycles and the trains. They all took advantage of the wonderful facilities the inn offered. They danced, ate and drank and left the passengers in the cattle cars, it was mid July of 1942."

Suzannah gave me the impression that she was not very fond of Monique or I may have imagined it because of my own conclusions.

"According to Monique, the officers and also lower level SS soldiers met plenty of women; some had mistresses with them. They all enjoyed a good time, music, good food and plenty of alcohol. While all this was going on, the Jews being transported were left in the cattle cars."

Suzannah changed demeanor as she told me this story about passengers without hair and cramped into compartments like sardines. For the first time, she sounded angry. She even suggested, based on the route Monique talked about, she knew where the Jews came from and where they ended up.

"Monique described the atmosphere around the train without feeling. The people were not allowed to get out of the train and that was all. Babies were crying and the smell was very bad. Monique felt disturbed by lamenting voices because they interfered with the time she enjoyed with her friend. *De l'eau s'il vous plaît,* was a general, cry repetitively because they were all thirsty. Her father or the officers would not allow water. They were Jews. He did not like them because the Fuhrer did not like them. She did not tell us how her friend felt but we knew it did not matter. The fate of the people was set when they stepped on that train. I knew the same was occurring elsewhere but because Monique who was there was telling the story, I felt anger.

"Suzannah, how did you react to such a story? Did you not want to know more details?"

Suzannah looked at me a long time and reminded me there was nothing she could do and also, Monique was a pathetic young girl who wanted to impress others. She took the time to remind me not to judge. Suzannah told me she knew what the fate of the passengers was to be. She said she had grown accustomed to such stories and continued to tell me the story. Monique was not allowed to take her cat Minou when she came to the South of France.

"Suzannah, why was this Monique where you were? I do not understand. And what about the cat?"

"Because she had to be sent away for her own protection. It was in Lyon that Monique's uncle and his wife resided. They did something heroic and it caused their arrest by a group of SS soldiers and some French gendarmes. While Monique's immediate family collaborated with the Germans, the uncle and his wife had joined the resistance and were helping Jews to safety. There was a Jewish doctor in their dark attic, which was why Monique's uncle and wife were arrested. The doctor was taken to a labor camp. Soon after, sick and overworked, we were told he died there. I do not know what happened to the uncle or his wife, but in most cases they would have been dispatched to a camp or killed on the spot. Monique did not say what took place after the arrest. I know she never saw her aunt and uncle again. A neighbor, afraid for her life took her to the convent. We never asked too many questions of each other; we knew the answers were hard to articulate and too painful to absorb."

"You know, Suzannah, I am glad I was not around, I do not think I could handle such times."

Suzannah took me in her arms and with the sweetest tone told me she too was glad I was not around then.

"Monique was both sweet and strange. She cried a great deal and since we each had plenty to cry about, we felt her tears were private. The nuns were strict but good people. They could sense something peculiar about Monique. They knew she missed her parents as we all did but they sensed something more. She had a brother and for some reason she never talked about him. We did not know if he was dead or alive. With everything going on, life may have been too structured at the convent and Monique did not fit in with us. Somehow, providence has a way of making small miracles. One day she found a kitten behind the church. He was almost dead from starvation. There was an immediate transformation in her, so the cat was her savior. The nuns allowed her to keep it. We all played with Minou Deux. He was a great source of comfort for all of us. We played with that cat in the dark of night; his eyes reflected any light if there was any. I told you it was forbidden to have the gaslights on at night. The candles and the oil lamps were never used. We woke up with the sun, and our activities ended at sunset. You may consider this to have been ridiculous but it was necessary for the convent to be dark. The hope was bombs would not fall on our heads. Anyway, when we went to church for mass, the cat was kept in a basket in the attic where we had cots. Minou Deux knew his place and so did we."

Suzannah looked sad and sometimes tears filled her eyes, but she had a way of controlling herself or any tears from escaping. One day I asked her if the stories made her sad, why tell them? "Just forget about them!" I said.

She extended her arms toward me in an embrace. Caressing my hair, she said in a low tone, "I tell you these stories so you will know what happened in this world you were born into and the stories that remain after a war. The stories that make people who they are. People who survived attempt to construct some sense out of horrific events. They must live and move on which is not always easy! To my way of understanding, there is nothing a mind can construct to justify what happens during war. I cannot comprehend why any human would have an innate need to create fear, instill pain and destruction including methods of murdering for simply the sake of killing or eliminating in what ever way they could. The memories I have will be with me always. They are part of who I am. I may not tell you my stories with the clarity you would want but know it is my way of painting a fragment of your canvas for others to see. Matters of war have an effect on people. All people, Julienne! I tell you so you can never forget because whether you know it or not, you are part of the story."

"So what happened to Monique?"

"She stayed with us and after the liberation when her brother came, he had been looking for her for a long while. They went back to where they came from. He was missing a leg; perhaps he too was a casualty of war. I never heard from her after that. I was told many who collaborated with the Germans were targeted. Some were jailed because they caused others to die. Some had their heads shaved; perhaps they would know what Jews felt. They were, however, not going to labor or death camp and hair grows. I do not know how they felt. I do not know what happened to Monique or her family. I do not even know what happened to the bones of my family."

I never gave any thought to such things, but Suzannah had her method to raise my awareness. She was successful and may not have known it.

"You have no idea how hard this period in history was. People stole from one another just so they could feed themselves or their families. Others told where Jews were hiding so they would be safe. The nuns rescued people like myself and I never asked why. Perhaps it was the Christian thing to do, or maybe it was an effort to have a larger Catholic base. It was my destiny not to end up in a gas chamber; it does not matter what the reasons were. Looking at you today is all the reason I will ever need in my life to be alive."

Suzannah told me so many stories and every time I opened the blue door, I checked to see what she had on her kitchen counter. Once inside, I could smell the vanilla even before I could see the cookies cooling on a tray. She baked for me, just for me, I was convinced, because she hardly ate any cookies. That day when I walked into the kitchen, I came back with two cookies, one for her and one for me. After that, I sat to hear more. Suzannah smiled.

"Those of us who were rescued were all so grateful! Without help, I know I would not be alive today. While we were at the orphanage, a convent they called it — our meals were nutritious, but not the best of taste. We were well nourished; we had thick soups made with fish bones, cabbage and other vegetables when they were available. We had three chickens and they were worth their weight in gold. The eggs they laid were part of our Sunday breakfast. After mass we had omelets with more vegetables, cream, and sometimes cheese and wonderful breads. Toward the end of the war, often a black car with well-dressed people came to visit and talk to us. We got to know them because they returned often with many gifts for us. Soon after the liberation people from La Croix Rouge came to visit us. They needed to know where we came from, the names of our families and so on. There was a search for families in the hope that we could be reunited with them. Alas, none of us at the convent had any family left. Since we were in a fishing village some nuns who liked to fish did so from under a pier. I had inside duties so I did not fish and really had no desire to. The nuns deboned the fish for sale, and the rest became part of our soup. In our enclosed yard we had sheep. We used the milk from the two females to make cheese for sale and we kept some for special occasions. The nuns were able to buy some things including medicine, on the black market. They visited the old people who often were sick from malnutrition. The driver in the black car I told you about brought some sulfa and other medicines. I had inside duties, I was the one putting the small jars and miniscule little boxes made of paper in place in the dispensary. The nuns were ingenious and industrious; they sometimes exchanged fish for other foods or cloth with which to make our garments. This went on for about two years during the war. One day a new command made it impossible to fish. Sister Anne and the others could no longer go fishing. It was something they thoroughly enjoyed, perhaps something that made them forget about war. We never knew who was watching. No one could be trusted and no one could be tempted. A disobeyed order was life threatening. The war machine had taken the goodness out of many people and made them into predatory monsters. Everything was done in fear, and when someone was caught doing something unacceptable to the Germans there was an execution or a disappearance. I can tell you, the little cat was a godsend. Minou Deux made us laugh and because of it, we were still able to express love. Deux as I called her, gave us a sense of hope for normal things. Monique did not take it with her when her brother came. That little creature kept us sane."

Suzannah never told me the last names of the people she talked about. I wondered if it was like when she was travelling from one place to another. "Better not know! Less dangerous that way," she often said.

I told Frank this story. He held my hands, kissed them and said, "Suzannah must have been a very special person; I have a sense she must have loved you very much. I see how you are looking at me. Julienne, my darling, I think between the polish you received from your mother and Suzannah's stories, I ended up with a wonderful woman."

The wind shifted all I could think of was how much I missed these interludes.

A Need For Friends

I had the flu and after four days I was so dehydrated I had to be hospitalized. It was good that I had befriended Jennifer and James. They not only took care of my garden but James also fixed anything broken around the house. Jennifer was the one who decided I needed to be hospitalized; she saved my life, something I will remember always.

My stay at the hospital brought to mind Frank's last day in France. He wanted his ashes brought back to America and this was not an easy task. Being hospitalized in the USA felt fine and made me realize I had a few things to take care of. The nurses and doctors were gentle and concerned because I had no relatives. I will never know how Frank felt about being in a hospital in France. I was always allowed to be with him for as long as I wanted. His being a terminal condition, it was important to be there until the last peaceful minute. I am thankful for that. This simple interaction with a hospital brought me to the realization, new friends would have to be made to replace the family I no longer had. Jennifer was becoming family and I was happy about that.

One nurse named Monika who had befriended me suggested I come to her home for Christmas. I accepted the invitation and when I asked her how many people were invited, she said only me. She had no husband or any close relatives and she felt we would enjoy the dinner she intended to cook. I had something to look forward to and presents to buy. If Monika felt sorry for me, it did not matter. My American family was growing. I was going to treat her and Jennifer like the angels they were.

Recovered after days of intravenous feeding, I was mulling over the story Suzannah told me about Monique. I could not fathom not giving water to people caged in the cattle cars. Suzannah could have decided not to tell me the entire story because usually she only talked about what she had experienced and there is something to be said for that. I must accept the reality that I will not be able to verify most of her stories.

"Pay attention, Julienne" was an admonition I heard often and I am glad, by the time I met Frank I had learned the art of listening.

Having been dehydrated, I could relate to the sensation of a thirsty body. I only had the flu. Hospital and doctors were available to me with their intravenous feeding tubes and I could get a drink of water whenever I wanted. I kept thinking about the people in the train outside of Monique's parent's inn. It is hard to accept that I am part of this humanity.

In the summer of 1942 France made it possible for over 13,000 Jews to be transported to the Vélodrome d'Hiver. Le Vent Printanier they called it. A round up, in occupied France to eliminate as many Jews as possible. At the Vélodrome there was no water and after the long days there, the women and children were taken to Auschwitz to be gassed. My hope is that this girl named Monique did not know. I hope she was only ignorant and not indifferent to the plight of the people in cattle cars. My prayer is that she did not know what was going to happen to the people. The station she talked about was along the fatal route. Monique resided where few people with yellow stars were ever seen. Was she too young and oblivious to the events around her to know what was going on? Was she conditioned not to care? How could such things happen?

In a moment of utter repugnance I got up wishing to feel the harbor's breeze. This time I took Frank with me. All along his ashes were in a box in my bedroom. Carrying the rosewood box made at a factory in France, I hoped a new phase of my life would begin. Walking down my seven steps to the driveway, I crossed the road and continued to the beachfront, less than half a mile away, wearing his fisherman sweater. Walking and trying to feel connected to the waves, the water and the air Frank could no longer breathe was enough to give myself permission to release to the sea what this man had wanted when he was alive.

A grandfather was walking in my direction and two young children with him were searching for seashells. A polite hello made me realize how different he was from Frank. He did not engage me in conversation. A few more steps, I smiled, my rosewood box, now empty and lighter, held no sentiments. I had released my husband to the waves that came calling.

Each step I took, brought Suzannah closer. The stories she told me had taught me compassion. I walked, the wind flirting with my hair, I became aware I had to make room for another side of who I was.

Within a few seconds I was once again wondering if it was possible that Monique's parents were scared. Their inn had been turned into a paradise for the SS. Were her parent's collaborators because they did not like or hated Jews? Were they trapped and were merely survivors? These and many other questions would have to remain unanswered. It was time to walk back home.

The waters in the harbor sang a different song and I continued to wonder how many died because they had no water. According to Suzannah, Monique heard the moaning and the crying for water. "De l'eau s'il vous plait." A long time ago I had read it was a particularly hot summer. I question how I would have felt if in similar circumstances. Would I have wanted sustenance to live one more day? Would I tell my story if I survived or would I carry the burden alone? Would anger dictate my attitude? Time, I imagined, had its way of healing. Suzannah was not angry although pain was an intimate friend. She told me to learn to remember incidents but also to learn to forgive. Suzannah was a special woman with capacities I may not have.

The 1979, Thanksgiving was very wonderful even with people I did not know. I had had one such holiday with Frank so I knew what to expect. I brought a special cranberry relish made with fresh cranberries boiled in a good red wine and some brown cane sugar. To this concoction I added walnuts, apple chunks and I grated orange rinds and also added some of the juice. Everyone present seemed to like my dish. None of the guests had ever socialized with a French person. It was a pleasant afternoon. From this group, I made some friends. How wonderful it was for James and Jennifer to invite me. I will reciprocate next year with other new friends. An American Thanksgiving with a French twist. I think my guests will enjoy it. Best of all I had a year to plan. In a festive mood I was almost ready for Christmas with Monika.

The weather was cooperating. I could still spend hours on the porch rocking my memories into submission. I made tea in the morning and drank it at room temperature the rest of the day. I seemed to be obsessed with the story about Monique. Could this girl have been talking about the 13,000+ Jews who were arrested under the cover of darkness from Paris in 1942? I had met a woman whose family was taking away; they were Jews from Turkey who had immigrated to Paris. She was young during that dreadful summer, and she escaped Auschwitz because her parents felt danger lurking had arranged for her to be taken away by friends. This young girl, though Jewish by birth, became a Catholic. Many such stories have been verified. French soldiers and gendarmes arrested their compatriots because they were Jews and the occupying Germans had given the order. Did the French military and the people of France feel they needed to reduce the Jewish population? Could it be they were concerned only with self-preservation? Was everyone scared and following orders to the letter? I was scandalized and yet aware that during the course of a war, people did die regardless of cause or reason.

Telling me stories, while offering me pieces of pie she made, Suzannah was a teacher of a period in history that would become part of my curriculum if I ever got the position at the college. If I take this job as a history teacher, will I measure up to the standards that Suzannah set before me? This woman taught me so much, yet, at the time, I did not capture the true value of her words. Why I continue to wonder does it take so long to digest. I want to continue the teaching she began. As her student I was engaged in my own reveries but what I retained I knew I could teach. When I heard these stories, I was young, foolish and too engaged in my own life, as students of mine might be. The idea will be to capture something within each that would leave a mark. Suzannah did that. Decades later I question the behavior of mankind. "Pay attention," Suzannah said thousands of time. I read the news and people with different faces continue to be slaughtered everyday. I wish I could have verified the Monique story but there was no way since Suzannah had no records, only haunting memories of a story. The telephone rang, it was Jennifer, and she wished to stop by. I felt a cup of tea, some cookies and small talk was in order. We were becoming good friends.

The Caribbean

At 9:30 AM I heard the gate being opened. Three minutes later, in her jeans and a peasant style blouse, looped earrings and a scarf flowing down to her knees Jennifer got out of her car. She was beaming, excited beyond words, she announced they were taking a trip to the Caribbean. Married five years James surprised her with the tickets. They were first going to New York for two days and then planned to continue on to a Caribbean vacation. It was more than a wedding anniversary; it was also to celebrate her birthday. While away she would turn twenty-five.

"Julienne, we got married on my birthday. James is bad with dates; he was the one to pick the date because he felt I would remind him of my birth date but not our anniversary. So, now he has only one date to remember. Clever, hey?"

She reminded me of myself every time something special was happening in my life, especially when I was in my twenties. That was not too long ago and I still can remember. We talked about her expectations of the various islands. She was determined to sample all rums produced on the island and taste all the coffees. Alas, Bermuda was the only destination. Her morning visit was meant to convince me to go shopping with her. She had a clear agenda. She said, liking the way I dressed, she wanted my advice because she wanted to buy a few dresses to wear while away. A couple of pairs of sandals were also part of the probable purchases. I was to be her fashion advisor and we were to travel to the next town to a series of shops she loved. Flattery worked, and I had not seen all of Knox County. Without hesitation, I accepted the invitation. As we talked and shopped, I learned a great deal about her and she about me. Later that evening I took her to dinner.

We found a small Cuban restaurant Jennifer knew about it from friends. The place reminded me of this story I told her.

"I visited Cuba right after a revolution changed the government there. I will bet the owners of this place are here as a direct result of that revolution. I went there because of these events and the fact that the life of some people had changed. My father helped people before I was born. Some Jews moved there during and right after WWII and once more wanted to relocate. They were from Europe, primarily Germany and Poland. I was on vacation so I went along. Suzannah was with me. My father, who had been involved in getting these folks there during the war, was again helping them with other residences. They were Jews and they had escaped Hitler's wrath. For me, it was an opportunity to visit a part of the world I had not seen, much like what you are about to do during your vacation."

"Julienne, I do not understand. Why was your father involved? Are you Jewish?"

"I am not, but my father had a notion that he could help because he had relatives involved in the resistance. He was in a position and also was of the belief that he could help. He facilitated passage on boats that were built where we lived. It is a complicated story. The problem, as I understand it, was many countries were afraid to have Jewish people arriving on their shores. These people ended up in the Caribbean. I knew nothing about this until I took the trip. My mother did not want me to go because of the perceived political danger. She was sick and probably would not have gone anyway. My father said it was okay for me to be with him, so I went. Suzannah, oh I never told you about her, she lived in a little house behind the one we lived in. Whenever my parents were away, she took care of me so she was almost like a mother to me. She was also one of my teachers. Anyway, she had a friend in Cuba and travelled with us. Suzannah was my very best friend and on this trip, she was my chaperon. Had she not traveled, I am sure Maman would not have allowed me to go anywhere. Though I do not think she was enamored with Suzannah, she trusted her and knew she would look out for me. The arrangements were perfect. My dad was busy with meeting Jewish folks and I visited from museum to the wonderful beaches."

"Oh my word, I had no idea your family was involved in world intrigues."

"I do not know about world intrigues. All I know, like you, was that I was going on an adventure. The whole thing about people relocating did not interest me, I just wanted to visit places I had never been to, have fun. The Caribbean and the Mediterranean seas are not the same."

"Didn't you come from Paris?"

"I lived in Paris with Frank when we were married. But I was born in a place called Toulon. Like here we were close to water."

I told her she would meet artisans in open markets selling their crafts, some masters and some amateur each producing astonishing art. I saw small and large paintings representing Cuban environment. She was getting excited at the prospect; she wanted a wooden bowl and a small watercolor.

"I purchased a small painting because the artist's brush captured the sky, and the colors he used kissed and captivated my soul."

"How did you know you would like it for more than the duration of your trip?"

I did not have a precise answer for her, but explained it was more a feeling, not knowing with any assurance. Just knowing for sure I wanted that painting around me.

"Do you remember when I asked you if you knew a framer? I kept his name, went to visit his shop and had him reframe my small painting. It is the one between the two bookcases directly facing the front door. The next time you come in, take a good look. It is a masterpiece."

It was the first time I thanked her. The framer was an artist himself and we enjoyed our conversation. His work was superb, and I thought perhaps one day we would be friends.

"I bet you will return with treasures of your own. While in the islands make sure you taste coconut water. I drank gallons of it. The natives make a hole with a sharp machete and hand you this large fruit with a straw."

"Did you put rum in it?"

"No, no one told me about that. I was too young to dream of it and Suzannah would not have allowed me any rum. Anyway, the day I tasted coconut was the afternoon we visited Mrs. Hilda Goldberg. She was an old friend of Suzannah's and was going to move to the Dominican Republic with her husband who looked like he never had a meal. You know, he never talked the entire time we were there. Suzannah was happy to see Hilda. When we got to her house, she offered us what I believe was a kind of dumpling soaked in Cuban rum covered with crushed sweet almonds. Wherever you go, make sure you get that dessert. I believe it is readily available on all the islands. You will never forget it. Hilda offered us this dessert and tea; I would have preferred more coconut."

"Why did this woman need the help of your father to move somewhere else if she no longer liked where she was?"

"You know, I have no idea. Hilda looked capable of taking care of anything. She was a short woman, older than Suzannah. She did not know how to dress. When we visited her she wore a print with pink and yellow flowers larger than her head. Fashion was not something she cared about. I could not imagine her being a friend of Suzannah; she looked like a farmer with hair on her chin. The two women spoke for hours in German. Hilda did not speak French well and Suzannah did not speak Spanish. A stack of magazines from all over the world kept me occupied during the visit. At least you will not be doing any of that during your vacation. The husband spoke not a word, just hello when we came in. Every time I looked at Hilda, I could not help but think about the presents Suzannah got for her. We all do this sort of thing from time to time. We do not see people for eons and in our mind we create an image that is not accurate. Suzannah bought her two silk blouses, at least three sizes too small, a beautiful cashmere shawl, and candles she made herself. After meeting Hilda I knew the blouses would not fit and there was no way this woman would wear cashmere. Later on in the evening, when we were alone, Suzannah said it was the intention and gesture that held meaning, not what I thought."

"What adventures you had!"

"I must say your gesture of this morning to invite me on this excursion is the type of intention Suzannah was talking about. You too bring joy to others. I am not buying any clothes and I am having a good experience because of you."

"Did you stay at Hilda's home?"

"No, we stayed at an old inn in Havana. I think it was originally built as palace around 1876. At least, this is what we were told. Are you and James going to stay in large hotels or old colonial small ones?"

"James got the airline tickets but we have not yet made up our minds about a place to stay. We are only going to Bermuda for a few days. You were lucky to go to many islands."

"Mine was a long journey; we were in Cuba a few days, than continued to Jamaica and the Dominican Republic where my father was to arrange housing for many people. Suzannah said he knew how to do these things because he had been doing this since the war. I loved the island breeze and for the days we were there I took a nap almost every afternoon. The evening dining was an event complete with music and dancing. The food was different and tasty and the people colorful and very friendly. You will find this out when you go. Try the traditional foods, and dance! Suzannah said I could have been a native of Cuba when I was dancing."

"Did you and Frank dance a lot? When you talk about him I feel he must have been a very special man. I am sorry you did not have a long marriage or a child —— look at this dress, do you think I would look good in it? Maybe one night James will take me dancing."

"Try this one too. It looks wonderful and will show off the tan you will get. If you do not go dancing, make sure you go for a walk at night; you will see millions of stars. After a while they will appear close enough to touch. There is a kind of night bird in the islands. I swear one sang for me every night I was there."

"Jennifer, you look wonderful, allow me to buy this dress for you and these sandals too.

"You don't have to buy the dress or the sandals for me, I can pay for them."

"I know you can pay, but if I buy them, you will have more money to spend in Bermuda."

"Thank you, this is so nice. I now have three dresses, two pairs of sandals. I am set."

"So, dear friend, let us go get something to eat, it is getting late and I am starving."

It took no time at all to find the place. The husband was Italian and the wife Cuban. What a coincidence that was. We were having a wonderful meal and drinking an Italian red wine. Jennifer asked me if I knew any stories about this woman named Hilda.

"Hilda's mother and father were Jews from Turkey. They had been arrested early in 1942. One night when Hilda was sleeping at her girlfriend's, SS and also some French gendarmes put the entire family on a train bound to a concentration camp or a crematorium. Hilda woke up at her girlfriend's but never again saw them. Her older sister was taken the next day when she was attempting to break into their home. The front door had been padlocked. Hilda felt her sister might have wanted to get coats and boots to survive the winter. Hilda was saved that day. She had been playing at a neighbor's house. Suzannah told me Sarah was never heard from again. If I understood correctly, Hilda's family had made arrangements with a Catholic family they knew well who lived up the street. The adults knew something evil was going on. Hilda was soon taken to another place to people she did not know, and they kept her in an attic. This was a lonely but the only place where she could be safe. Food was scarce and she received very little. Her friend could not come and visit; she said she never saw her again. When Suzannah told me the story I felt so sad for all of them. A seven year old could not have understood why she had to hide. During our visit, Hilda mentioned the fears her rescuer must have experienced. She lived with eight different families and for the safety of her rescuers she was to remain in the shadows. She looked too Jewish, and in Germany during that time, it took very little to lose one's life."

"Do you know where this happened?"

"In Germany but Suzannah did not tell me what town. I can tell you this is not a singular story. There were heroic rescuers no one knows much about. Suzannah told me in one of the homes the family's son molested Hilda more than once. As most molesters, he told her he would kill her if she said anything. This is a common practice employed by tormentors of many kinds. Hilda said as bad as he was he sometimes brought her slices of apple or bread with butter. She cried when she was telling us; she felt lucky to be alive yet, at times, wished she were dead. 'Memories, they stay with you,' she said many times. The boy was killed soon after he joined a division of the army. He was sent to Poland and according to Suzannah, Hilda felt guilt for feeling glad he was dead, and relief for knowing he would not molest her again."

"I do not think guilt would have been what I felt. You know, there is a lady in town. I heard she was a survivor of WWII, I do not know her, I've just heard about her. I am told she is old and owns a store. I will get the name and address for you. Maybe you should meet her. Maybe she is Jewish and knows stories too."

Jennifer had a good dinner, but thinking of Hilda and telling the story took away my appetite. The aroma of my dish assured me that all was delicious. I pretended to be feeling a bit out of sorts. I had the food put in a box to have later on. I was upset because of the conversation we were having. I should have changed the subject but did not. Our evening together progressed and it was late when we were done. We left the restaurant and headed home. Jennifer bought a bread pudding for James. It was a fun day even if part of our conversation did not seem necessary. The drive home took about two hours. I had not realized we had ventured so far.

Once at home, I continued to think of Suzannah who believed cleaning a kitchen was great therapy when upset about things she could not change. Cleaning imaginary particles of dust seemed like a good idea. Any unrealistic expectations of the world could be scrubbed away.

It turned out, cleaning the kitchen administered a good doze of healing. My kitchen, the heart of my home and my own inner heart, were both in need of a good scrubbing. As I scrubbed away, I could almost hear the attic noises where Hilda was kept. The room itself was lined with books. The grandmother of the young man read to her and she learned to read because of this lady. Hilda became a reporter. After the war she wrote books and newspaper articles. She married and continued to write until her husband got too sick and she took care of him. I did not see books or magazine articles written by her when I was at her home. I was tired and ready for bed; I could not bear to think about more people with such courage.

I picked up a notebook I had placed in one of the bookcases; it was a handwritten manuscript Frank had left unfinished. I read it out loud as if I could hear his voice instead of mine. Soon I fell asleep.

The next day a yellow bus delivered school children on the corner. They, of course, did not have yellow stars on their clothes. They were safe and going home without a worry in the world. I had never before thought about children going or coming from school.

Something so simple brought home the fact that I had no children of my own to hold dear. If Frank were still alive, I would at least be pregnant by now, and if Suzannah were here with me, I think I would say I had a charmed life.

After the day with Jennifer I realized I no longer wished to spend the rest of my life with the notion that memories of old would miraculously change my life. It became obvious that I had the responsibility to make the changes needed. I could no longer postpone living fully.

Back from the Islands

For reasons I could not explain I was thinking about my vacation in the Caribbean, Perhaps being with Jennifer had something to do with it.

I returned home from this island vacation with gifts for my mother, a mantilla I obtained from an old woman at an outdoor market in Cuba made a hit. She told me her own mother had one almost identical. The lace was beautiful with flowers and around the edges each petal was re-embroidered with black, white and gray silk. Fringes of the most radiant mercury color complemented the side edges of this rather long headdress. Though Maman said her mother had a similar one, she did not seem overly exited about it. In retrospect, at that time my mother did not seem to ever get exited about the things I did or why I did them. This may have been one reason why I spent so much time with Suzannah. With my mother I felt as an outsider trying to get in. Mother was a difficult woman. I think she felt cheated because everyone who knew my family thought I looked exactly like my father. It is possible that she secretly wanted me to look and behave like her. Often this feeling bothered me but we did not talk about it. She examined my purchases. For me, the best was a record of local music for me. Maman was pleased with that, she was thinking of culture until she heard what I was dancing to. More often than not, Maman did not understand me. In Jamaica I got her some pressed flowers made into a bookmark. The dried flowers were pressed into the larger leaves of a plant I did not recognize. They were glued and received coats of shellac. This present had the desired effect, and she even recognized the flower petals as being rare orchids from South America. I was pleased to see my mother's broad smile framing perfect teeth, a smile as rare as the orchids. When I told Jennifer I did not investigate every corner of the Dominican Republic, she was surprised. I told her how sick I had gotten when we arrived there after our Cuban and Jamaican stops. I reminded her to be careful with what she ate, but particularly the local waters. She was surprised but accepted my suggestion. This was the first time I had to be hospitalized. A most unpleasant experience two days before going home and I think Jennifer got the point.

Talking about this Caribbean trip with Jennifer brought other memories to the surface. It was not clear to me why some people my father had helped years before needed additional assistance. The ones I met were all people of sound mind and body. Suzannah said it was because they felt he saved their lives. There is so much I may never understand or know. There was a disturbance; my gate at the end of the driveway had an alarm and I heard it.

The yellow bus pulled away and I saw one boy as he opened the gate. He walked the driveway to my home. When he saw me on the porch, he stopped,

"Mam, you're going to think I'm crazy, but I have a bet with some kids and the teacher in my French class. You are the French lady who lives here now, right!"

"Yes, I am this French person. What can I do for you, and what was your bet?"

"In our French class, we need a real French person to talk to us a little so we can get the words right. My mother heard you when you spoke to a woman at a store and told she me about you. I told my teacher. So, I figure if you came to the school and talked to us we could hear how you talk and we would be able to say the words better. My teacher said if I could get you to the school it would be okay with him. Everybody in the class made a bet and said it would not happen. They said that you would throw me out of your house if I ever dared come in and ask. I don't want to lose the bet and I'm running for class president and I want to learn French. What do you say, Mrs. Fairchild?"

He knew my name. The boy had at least looked at the name on the post.

"I think you won the bet. I can come and talk to your classmates and your teacher. You make the arrangements and I will be there."

"You mean it! Can I tell Mr. Rand?"

"You may tell him. I will give you my telephone number. Have him call me and we will schedule a time. I will be honored to meet your classmates and your teacher."

He scaled my seven steps in record time. In the library I took pen and paper and wrote my name and telephone number. It took him three seconds to disappear. Pleased with this encounter, I went back to my reveries, realizing I did not know the boy's name. For some reason another thought came crashing.

We were home a few days when Father became very sick with an intestinal malady, something similar to what had put me in the hospital. The doctor did not seem to know what to do. He called in a colleague who administered something new to my father. He felt better for a few days, but then relapsed. This time, whatever was wrong, was deadly. Within a few days, I watched my father's health deteriorate drastically. Some strange and unknown bacteria to the doctors overwhelmed the medications that were being given to him. Mother was worried. She spoke to no one and we all stayed away from her. Suzannah had long conversations with me about appreciating the things we had and accepting the things we were not able to change in our lives.

Refusing to accept her words, I persisted with the business of being alive. I had no idea she was preparing me for a life-changing event.

Life at home was no longer like it had been. My mother assumed the reins at this time. She allowed me one hour with my father everyday. Those hours were divided into four fifteen-minute segments because he could not handle more. I woke up from an absolute slumber. All was still. The day before my father told me he loved me and wanted me to have a good time with life and to live it fully. I felt all was safe.

The grandfather clock from England chimed at 3:15 A.M. It was February 12, 1964. At the funeral, my mother wore the Mantilla from Cuba. I guess it was appropriate with her black dress with long sleeves. Other black dresses she wore were cocktail dresses. He was gone and in her mind it was appropriate to wear long sleeves; her husband was dead. I too was dressed in black with short sleeves. Suzannah was in dark blue. Aunt Erika visibly distraught also wore black. The entire house, once a place of laughter, had become one where eyes looked glazed and feelings were unspoken.

I spent the rest of the day in the guesthouse with Suzannah while people I did not know came to offer their condolences. No one talked much that somber afternoon of the funeral. I fell asleep with my head on Suzannah's lap. We were sitting on her sofa and she was caressing my hair while talking to me. Aunt Erika brought us some cucumbers and smoked salmon. I was not hungry. I took refuge in a fetal position with a colorful shawl covering me.

A Breeze

As a final warning, the wind blew violently, announcing winter around the corner! The breeze was cold and my only thought was how I would spend hours on my rocker, watching, remembering, smiling or sometimes crying.

I had grown accustomed to my reveries thinking about Suzannah or Frank. My friendship with Jennifer had grown, but our age and cultural differences were clear to me and I think evident to her. Venturing to various stores and little boutiques had become a pleasurable pastime but I was no longer mesmerized by the content of any stores, nor were they a magnet to attract new friends. I was taking some classes at the local college. The people I met in class were interesting and from various parts of the world, but all too busy to pursue any friendship; most I found out would not remain the entire winter. People in this part of the globe were always busy. This, too, was a cultural difference. People in France always made time to meet and chat and have a good time. So far it was obvious I had not met anyone willing to make time for the simple pleasures brought on by conversation. Frank told me about these divergences, and perhaps this was why he enjoyed Paris. He was a raconteur and people were willing to listen. The people here were different and my task, I concluded, I was to make attempts to understand them. At first I thought the café au lait Frank drank by the gallon made it

155

possible to talk to people he encountered in various establishments. So, like him, I went to a little cafe in town where I soon noticed people drank their coffee without conversing with others. How different they were. Forced to withdraw, I went back to my porch where I wished someone would drop by and begin a conversation about anything at all. With no one around to tell, my decision was made in an instant. Somehow, I would duplicate an environment where people would gather at my home to talk, to discuss and discover the feeling of aliveness. They would do so in the dead of winter in front of a warm blowing fireplace. I will find art and letters all around me; I was in the right part of the USA. I just had to find the right people.

My first invitation would be extended the next time someone talked to me. The first five words would lead to an invitation to share a café-au-lait. I promised myself to ask this person to bring a friend or two and explain why. Thus would begin a new salon type gathering at my home. I knew it was possible because people are the same everywhere no matter how busy they think they are.

Another gust and the breeze escalated to a freezing wind that reminded me I had shipped some of Frank's heavy sweaters. I had one in mind, made of heavy, off-white wool; he called it his fisherman sweater. The time had arrived to retrieve it from one of the boxes left unopened.

I walked to the guest bedroom where I still had three boxes left untouched. They were neatly stacked in the closet. My mother would have found this acceptable. She did not like to have clutter around her and obviously neither did I. This was a good day to explore and see what else I had not unpacked. The first box tagged KITCHEN opened with ease and inside I found my small espresso machine, my cheese knives with bone handles, our dessert plates purchased at an antique store not far from our apartment. There were a multitude of cloth napkins I did not remember having. I sat a moment on the floor looking at one of the plates perhaps to better savor the last piece of apple pie I had made for Frank. Before long, my plate empty as it was when I began my examination and left me unsatisfied. That day in Paris, I had my first and last attempt at pie baking. We were home that November and I had my first Thanksgiving experience. I cried in his arms when he talked about being thankful. We both knew his time was running out. As I cried for what I did not want to lose, Frank urged me to be grateful for what was happening at that moment between us and not what would happen in the future. He told me when he died his ghost would be around me for all eternity. Perhaps today he was looking at me. He was an astonishing man who accepted his mortality. He was serious when he made clear to me we needed to be grateful for what we had. Frank and Suzannah could have been twins; their conversations with me were almost interchangeable. Although this was not Thanksgiving Day I was thankful. I had experienced both sides of great love and intimacy.

From the window I saw a bird. He flew by and decided to land on my rocker. He looked like a gull. I took the napkins and the espresso machine to the kitchen. The dessert plates were in the dining room where I found the perfect place for them in my new cupboard. The bird's eye followed me; he moved when I did. He could see me from the windows. With little notice, he flew toward the sea. Perhaps a good day for fishing he had no need for a fisherman's sweater but I did.

This momentary reprieve was disrupted with another gust of wind. The rocking chairs kept moving back and forth; I thought of Frank. Perhaps he really was with me.

The larger box was my next choice. It had been taped at least three times by the moving company. After getting a knife and breaking the seal, I found myself looking at sweaters in a variety of colors. Frank was a sweater man.

As I examined each folded sweater, I soon realized some still held his scent. After pressing them a moment against my face, I refolded the first sweater with care. I opened the bottom drawers of the oak dresser I had purchased a week before. The room with its old furniture, all new to me was ready in case a guest arrived. Equipped with a double bed, two small tables from different antique stores. One was square the other round, each just large enough for not much more than a book. The driftwood headboard also from an antique store was almost gray with age. A painted seascape, not unlike the harbor I looked at every day, created a peaceful scene centered on the wall above the headboard. One lamp was too large for the table it sat on. It was a blue ceramic and for the moment did the job. One day soon I would take Jennifer with me and we would shop for two new lamps. The very large window had no draperies and the easel stood ready to receive its first canvas. The fisherman's sweater did not make it to the drawer. Although it was too large, I put it on. While folding back the sleeves to show my fingers, I wondered if Frank had ever gone fishing,

Phenomenal were the emotional attachments and sensations I experienced relating to Frank. Wearing the sweater confirmed that I did not know much about him. In retrospect, I knew love and our engagement in matters of living every moment to its full expression left me with something no longer physical yet still palatable. Occupied with his students in the same manner, I felt certain they missed him too. There was no one to consult about my understanding of love; it was unnecessary, I knew. I thought of my mother who never spoke of how she felt about anything. A reserved woman, Aunt Erika used to say. I wondered if she had known the kind of love I had discovered. Mysterious also were Suzannah's feelings; with no one to share these thoughts with, I could not shout, "I know what love is!" Suddenly, I felt depleted of vital forces. Looking toward the sea, I noticed the emptiness of the trees around my home. They were not completely depleted, there were branches with some leaves, but overall in disguise, I could already see the promise of spring. Each bud was awaiting a new beginning. The certainty of my own blooming was just around a curve, another invisible corner for sure. I knew it was there, awaiting my movement toward its discovery.

The telephone rang and on the line the French teacher was asking me to visit the classroom. Mr. Rand sounded pleasant and very grateful I had accepted the invitation and challenge Robert had dreamed up. I was happy to now have a name for this boy. We set the date, talked briefly about what was expected of me. The busy teacher, hang up. I went to my desk and put the date and time down on so I would not forget. Invigorated by this news I decided to go for a long walk.

Moments of reflection about those I loved brought to mind my turbulent life of many summers past. The chaos and disorder had gone out of me. For that, I was grateful. I continued to feel torn, it had been my choice to move here, still, there was something depressing and disheartening about being in a country where I knew no one. The prospect of meeting a classroom filled with student felt very well.

As I walked the beach my reveries ascended to higher grounds and I observed the pleasures I took for granted. The time had come to invite the few people I had met. Wishing to master the language would be the first and perfect excuse. My guest would go back home with satisfied appetites. Frank told me this was the method he used to get people to come to the apartment for conversation. American hot dogs, Coca Cola and beer were his standard fare. I knew I would do better with a coq-au-vin or some other food from my homeland. First I needed to decide on a full meal or simple appetizers. My new friends could have hot or cold dogs in their own homes. Our apartment in Paris was small but the dinner parties were successful. I will duplicate what I did in Paris. Once back at home, I would make the first phone call to Jennifer. I hastened home to make that call. After she accepted the invitation she suggested I also call Norma and her husband. By the second call all was in place. That Friday night we had a glorious dinner, lots of conversation and I did not even have to bake a pie. Norma and John enjoyed the meal. Like Jennifer and James, they had not been around people from other countries. We decided to find others and have an international salon series right in my living room. I praised them for their idea and put them in charge of finding the people they thought would be appropriate for what we had in mind. I discovered John was a veterinarian. We discussed the best type of dog I would do best with as a companion. Before leaving he told me he would find me the perfect dog. "One or two?" he asked as he closed car door. I am still trying to come up with the answer.

My first dinner was a success!

It Happened Too Fast.

It was just a few days before departure, Jennifer dropped by to make sure all was in order with me. We were developing a close friendship. She gave me a list of people I could call if I needed anything at all. This was a rather long list with the friends already met and new names too.

Jennifer wore her jeans again. I do not think I had ever seen her in a dress, except for the brief moments at the store, so I asked her about that.

"I wear a skirt when I go to church on Sundays. I am going to be dressed up 90% of the time during our trip. Did I tell you? We decided I would no longer take the birth control pills. Who knows, three of us may come back. Julienne, if I get pregnant would you consider becoming the godmother to my child? Like you, I have no family and we like each other. You are the person I would like closest to a child of mine. Besides, you can teach her French. You like me don't you?"

"Yes, I like you very much, it would be an honor to be a godmother. I think you will need to discuss this with James. I gather you would prefer a girl?"

"Girls are more fun. Maybe when you go visit friends in Europe one day, we can tag along."

"I never thought of going back; my memories of home are sad and I do not have much correspondence with my French friends. Distance and circumstances play these games on friendship. I only have two friends corresponding with me these days. In their last letter they each suggested they would love to see the USA. When you come back we will talk about your next vacation. Spring in Paris is something you would never forget. Anyway, Paris gave me the greatest love I could ever have experienced but the City of Light went dim one day. The whole of Toulon and its surrounding towns also became surreal to me. When I went to settle my parental affairs after my mother died, nothing looked or felt the same. The house, still filled with memories, left me with a cold and empty sensation. It was no longer home. Those were feelings that made selling the house relatively painless. It reminded me of the day my father died. No one talked, or else it was almost inaudible. The excitement and joy I had known my entire life had evaporated. The laughter of my father no longer surrounded my senses, nor did anyone else's laugh. I was alone, without my dear father there to take the lead I did not know what to do. This was the way it was at home. He was a jovial type of fellow; when he laughed it was infectious. When I went back before the sale of the house no musicians were in the kiosk and no one was there to serve coffee, I saw no cookies or cakes, not even for me. The dining room the table was there; the new owners wanted it. For some reason, it no longer felt a part of what I knew. The garden between the main house and

Suzannah's guest home felt as if it needed to be drenched. Every leaf looked gray. The birds did not seem to be singing their songs. This was not like any other Sunday. The wind blew but the pond's surface did not respond with a ripple. All was still around me. In my heart, happiness and turmoil had moved. The home had been in my family for over two hundred years. For these reasons, I do not have a desire to go back. Who knows things change? Perhaps I will take you to visit France. I will be your guide."

This was a sentimental moment with Jennifer.

"I cannot imagine living in a place so old. Our house is thirty years old and it feels like one hundred. I'm glad you are making major improvements here. I love what you did to the kitchen. Are you going to do something with the garden? So why did you not stay in Paris? By the way, you never told me about your dad. What kind of a man was he? I already know he spoiled you. I think James will be that kind of father specially if we have a girl."

"No one, except Suzannah, talked much about what my father may have been to them. Perhaps I was the single one who felt lost while the rest of the world moved on to a direction where I could not venture in. Even before he died, my mother never talked about my father, I am sure she loved him but kept feelings and any connections to herself. He was my hero and it took a long time for me to recover from his death. He was a jovial man who took on the ills of the world. He was not inclined to spoil me, at least not habitually. I remember him in a white suit and very colorful ties. I would play with his moustache when I was young. After he died, I think my world turned upside down. After he died, my mother was simply impossible to be around. Suzannah irritated her and so did I. When we talked with Aunt Erika she felt we were sharing secrets. It was a difficult time for all of us. Taking care of his affairs kept her busy. To me, she appeared angry. My father's death left me lost; my mother was unreasonable, but somehow we survived. You ask about the garden. I think next spring I will tackle a small garden, and maybe a pond, too. I will ask James what he thinks. I briefly mentioned it to him not too long ago."

"I am so sorry you had to go through all this. When my dad died, we all rallied. I met cousins I did not know, and that was a great comfort. I no longer see them but when they were needed, they were there. Anyway, this is old stuff. I want you to be my child's godmother. I know I will get pregnant soon."

"You are right, it is all old stuff. So hurry up and get yourself pregnant. I will think about people that influenced my life positively. Suzannah, the most significant, was the best teacher I ever had, I appreciate every word she spoke. So to you I say, if I am indeed the godmother to your child, I will protect it the way my father did and I will teach this child the things Suzannah thought me. You do realize this entitles me to spoil the kid! I also look forward to that."

"Wow, I wish I had people like that in my life. I am very happy but sometimes I get very scared. These days when James talks about a family, it scares the hell out of me. What if I am bad mother? I think you would be very good for my child. I would be less afraid if I knew my kids would not be alone."

"I already told you, I would be honored and would take care of your child no matter what."

A sign of relief covered Jennifer's face. Miraculously her fears vanished. I, on the other hand, felt the weight of the possible responsibility I had just assumed.

"Suzannah was a story teller. She told me so much I will never forget. I do not think I will bore your child with stories she will probably not care about. I can teach her French, how to paint, how to read and how to learn. It will be like taking your child to a daycare center."

She let me know this was not why she would be having a child. With a child, she no longer would work, at least until it was in school. She also told me not working was one of her fears. She never asked James for money.

"This makes perfect sense. There is a void in my life and an occasional child around me would work magic. I will appreciate this little person and I will teach that grandchild of mine all sorts of things."

"You said grandchild. I like that! We do not have our mothers, James and I. I think my child needs to know all your stories. How else can somebody like my child remember stories Suzannah told?"

"It was years ago when Suzannah told me to engage myself in whatever endeavors necessary to keep mind and soul occupied. This is exciting and the perfect time to heed to this advice. If you have a baby, I will follow your guidelines and be there for you and your child with mind, body and soul. I will fill every moment allowed with something valuable. I had been waiting for a magical wand. You my dear, hold that wand. Tomorrow I will go to the bookstore and learn about babies."

"Will you paint something for the baby's room?"

"Are you already pregnant? I can paint something for your baby's room. Do you know what you want? Better yet, I think you should do two things. Talk to James about it and wait and see if you have a girl or a boy. I think they like different things."

She was beaming, but it was time to go home. She did not walk to her car, it was more a bounce, and when she closed the car door I could see her broad smile. Jennifer was delightful!

My telephone rang, "Mrs. Fairchild, this is Arnold Rand, the French teacher. I was thinking it would no be a bad idea to meet. I would like to discuss how your visit to my classroom would go? Would you mind having a cup of coffee with me this Saturday? We could meet at the Main Street Coffee and Ice cream? It's kind of a halfway point for both of us."

Time was set for 10:00 AM and after this conversation I returned to my reveries of Suzannah and Frank but this time the pain was less poignant. The loneliness shifted; the love I felt for them remained intact but the prospect of a child around somehow changed something. Having something to do about teaching children was also an element that brought a pleasurable sensation.

I was waking from a long pause. Suzannah was right when she told me life was not mine to manipulate. Things happened in an order I did not anticipate. Somehow I retained her words; they all served me well. Soon enough, thinking about visiting France with Jennifer and a baby brought the images of my father's face. It took no time for his face to transform to that of a corpse. The father I loved soon left my world. The memories of him were still vivid; the same would happen with the memories of Frank. They were the men I had loved, differently, yet impossible to forget. I went into the guest bedroom to inspect the state of my paints still in a wooden box. To my surprise nothing had dried out. Everything was ready and waiting and I even had a blank canvas to stroke with my brushes. I soon would be painting something for a baby's room. I liked the idea.

Dancing with Paul

It was not long after a conversation with Suzannah, my heart still felt raw with pain. I decided I needed to escape. Joining friends at a dinner party given at a dance studio was what I needed. I drove my little Renault. I arrived late and dinner was over. That night, I wore a short royal blue dress with one bare shoulder. My dark hair was shinier than usual. My curls brought to the side of my covered shoulder made me remember my twenty-first birthday.

Suzannah did not comb my hair anymore; to my amazement, I had mastered the art. Mother did not like my attire but that was nothing new. Suzannah offered me a shawl. I took it but chose to leave it in the car. My high heels were higher than usual and walking the two hundred or so feet on the cobblestone path proved arduous. I thought of the thousands of times Suzannah had told me to pay attention. I had to watch where each step landed. Now marveling at the things able to make me smile, I questioned my judgment as I entered the hall where the party was underway. I was blinded with too much light and my ears were assaulted by noise and blasting music, too loud to think. A sea of people I did not seem to recognize was dancing. The strobe lights made me dizzy and excited all at once. Approaching me was a tall slim man in a dark suit. He was smiling and so was I. He was particularly well groomed and I liked that. He must have noticed me when I first walked in because he had two drinks in his hands. Without hesitation he offered me one. It was a Brandy Alexander. I never had one before and it tasted quite good. We talked for a long while and danced a lot. Our bodies synchronized to the rhythm and the strobe light. I was losing my way in his arms and I decided I needed to be home. I kept thinking about my father, my mother and Suzannah, too. Things Paul said or the way he held my hand when we danced created a longing I was ready to give in to. He walked me to my car; his was parked next to mine. What a coincidence! He too drove a Renault; his was red, an older model, he followed me home. He got out of his car and opened my door. For some reason I did not put my car in the garage on the side of the house. Paul suggested he would be visiting me in the very near future. He kissed both my hands, got back to his car and left. I felt a stirring and wished he had not gone.

I went straight to Suzannah's guesthouse. It was about two in the morning but she was up. The light in her living room was on. I had so much to tell her about Paul Deschamps. She listened to me without interruptions. When she brought me a cup of tea from her small kitchen, I heard her say:

"Julienne, at this time you are very vulnerable. Take time before you fall in love with this Paul. You do not know him. You know nothing about him. Listening to you, I am afraid you have made up your mind this man is meant to be part of your life. Take time to weigh how you feel. Take time to recover from your father's death." She took a sip of black tea while I protested.

"We talked all night, Suzannah. He told me things he never told anyone else. He is eloquent, tall, and handsome and no, I am not vulnerable. I am recovered from my father's death just fine. I even went to this party because I am fully recovered. You told me to live and that is what I am doing. It is almost two years since my father died. Paul made me feel so alive and I am going to see him and be with him. I feel it, I know it!"

"So, how old is Paul? Is he educated? Is he a professional? Is he from around here? What have you learned about these minor details? What do you know about him?"

Suzannah had an ability to irritate me. I got up and told her I was tired and went straight to my room. To her questions, I had no answers. I was very much aware of the stirring I felt when he kissed my neck and my hands. That was enough for me.

Those were not the feelings I had when I met Frank; my whole being wanted him in a more tender way. Paul had aroused only the primal in me, I did not care if he was an educated professional or what ever else Suzannah conjured.

Even as I was thinking of this episode, I kept caressing my various brushes. I could not help but laugh at the obvious significance of this.

173

When Life Changed Again

The porch continued to nudge me to think about my life. There was so much to sort out, so much to accept and ponder. Moving to other shores did not resolve the problems I travelled with. Days, weeks and months continued to flow out of me, and mental confessions presented little if any redemption. The guilt I once had seemed to be gone but residues of pain remained.

The death of my father, expected as it was, changed the things I took for granted. I could no longer expect the impossible. Mother, still angry at the world and with me, continued to search for reasons to argue and assert something within her. She had an argument with Aunt Erika who decided she would no longer reside with us. Maman had gone through her room and removed certain papers, mostly letters. Aunt Erika was angry but did not tell me what was taken out of her room. At home she had been part of the background, always there and ready to serve. This incident was more than Aunt Erika could endure, she moved to a convent where many older women were. She was not a nun nor very old. She told me she would be of service to the community. While she may have been fit for a cloistered life, I felt in our home she was of service to us all and seeing her go was heartbreaking. Every time I saw her after than she reminded me how much I looked like my father. Since his death she had become part of a circle around me. Mother was

175

jealous of anyone I got close to. Aunt Erika was the only surviving sibling of my father and a constant reminder that we had the same blood. I take consolation in the fact that I visited her once a week until she died only six months after her arrival at the convent. She had a massive stroke. Aside from my mother, I had no family. Suzannah the only sane person I knew.

Missing my father and missing my aunt, I knew Mother would not like or approve of any relationship with Paul who had become my lover. Suzannah had a piece of philosophy for everything and this case she believed life was not to be manipulated and we all had to get accustomed to change. On my porch and in my new home half a world away was evidence enough; I had grown accustomed to plenty of changes. How I could have thought Paul was the change I needed, I will never know. I knew without a doubt Maman and Suzannah would never approve of him. He was a substitute for a fire that had been extinguished in my life and became an alternate for the attention I received from my father. He was fun, passionate and I loved him. In the meantime, my quiet, unpretentious mother had turned into a tyrant. There was constant and growing tension between us. She was angry and, looking back I realize she may have been extremely fearful. I became aware of such possibilities after Frank died. For me there was great sadness.

I returned to the kitchen after examining a very large box containing more of my paints, brushes and palette knives. A cup of tea was in order. Suzannah made me tea whenever we were about to enter into dialogues in need of pauses. Sipping tea still helps me to better digest difficult things. My favorite cup was waiting for me; I poured myself a cup of Persian tea with cardamom. Paul re-entered my mind and I realized Mother's new persona might have been the easy excuse I needed to run into his arms. At that time I did not know how to reach her. It did not take too many cups of tea to see how pathetic this whole affair was.

As always, when I could not stomach a thought, my mind provided me with the perfect escape. Paul was the escape.

I remembered when Suzannah gave me her description of my father.

"He was a magnificent man, over six feet tall; his hair as curly as yours; he kept it a little long, like an artist would."

By the time I was born my father's hair was kept very short because I had no memories of him with long hair. I always thought he was a tall and magnificent man. Suzannah did not tell me anything I did not know.

The way she talked suggested she had a crush on him but we never discussed this possibility. I knew she never had an affair with him but there was something I did not know. Whatever it was I felt was the cause for Maman's dislike of Suzannah.

"Julienne, life can be unmerciful sometimes. There are always struggles. We must accept the things we cannot change because most of the time we have no choice. The simple reason is that some changes in our lives are not in our sphere of influence. The best thing is to be strong and go on. Most of all, we must learn about tolerance. Dear, you can change only what goes on between your ears." I am not sure what her reason was for these conversations. However, today, I have a clue; it is not tolerance that I battled with, it is acceptance.

"When I was young, because of such intolerance, millions of Jews were slaughtered. This entire subject is a lot more complicated than what I am saying to you right now, but believe me, people lost their humanity because they lost their sense of tolerance. Right now your mother is not tolerating people who were close to your father, perhaps because it causes her pain and she feels a need to exercise her newly found power. Perhaps she felt she tolerated too much for too many years. This could be why she asked Erika to move. My turn will come, too, I am sure of it."

Like millions of others, mother went through experiences foreign to her. We never know when a tornado will arrive at our front door. Suzannah knew and understood these life principles well.

"Life presents struggles. They seem to be conditions of life itself. How we surmount them depends on the choices we make. I try my best, and make all attempts not to hurt others with what I say or do. One accepts, one plows through, one finds levels of endurance we never suspected we had. Good use of the will, Julienne, is sometimes struggle enough. One can be happy and

178

content living with these principles because it is the most logical and reasonable way."

I do not remember when we had this conversation. She explained to me, when my father died and my mother became the mistress of the home she perhaps felt she was also the master of everything and everyone around her. It is conceivable she never gave any thought to what life without her husband would be like. Most people do not think about such things. In such instances we meet our demons, which are there to teach us. I am happy both Aunt Erika and also Suzannah were close to me and gave me a great deal of love. They were both more than just family and because of wishes my father might have had and that I know nothing about, mother may have felt crowded. She did not want them around. If this is correct, Mother spent years accepting things she could not change because she either loved my father or was afraid. It was not only my world that turned upside down; I was not alone, I am now sure of it. I was angry and selfish and did not comprehend that my mother could be distraught. If my theory is correct she too needed the time to accept facts as they were. Balance, I am finding, takes a great deal of work. She had too many pressures. I lifted the cup to my lips and drank more tea.

When Suzannah held me in her arms allowing me to cry, saying only how much she loved me and how grateful she was, it was enough that we had each other. She said we were each other's

179

light. Suzannah said many things to irritate my senses, but being each other's light was not one of them. Today, I miss that light.

Suzannah Must Go

It was an unusual and cold December day in 1965 when I opened the door to Mother's boudoir. She was sitting at her desk. Dressed in the black she had been wearing since the death of my father, her hair was pulled back in a bun and she wore no lipstick. The room had a foul aroma clinging to the old drapes and the Persian rug. She had taken up smoking which left me feeling nauseated. I was surprised to find Suzannah in the room, standing still; she smiled when I entered the room but said nothing.

It took only minutes and without asking Suzannah to sit, she looked at her and said, "Suzannah, you have lived here for over twenty years and the time has come for you to find another place. You will need to make some arrangements, but I know you have friends everywhere so this should not take more than thirty days. I feel this is a generous amount of time."

Suzannah, like a prophet, had told me that this would happen. Mother's half burned cigarette now in a full and putrid crystal ashtray, was done. I cannot erase from my mind how she looked at me turning her body to get a better view. By now Suzannah had left the room.

"You need to spent time in this house." My mother said. "Suzannah has a lot to do to facilitate her departure in due time. She does not need to be bothered by you every minute."

She lit another cigarette. Her conversation with me was over and required no retort. Like Suzannah, I had been dismissed. I felt something close to hatred toward my mother.

The night before I had prayed for joy and smiles all around me. My wishes and prayers had brought something quite different. I experienced a bitter reality and it chiseled a whole at my side. When I left my mother's boudoir, going to Suzannah was my only thought. She was walking slowly a short distance ahead of me. As she stepped on the large stones the path to her home looked dull. I ran and caught up. She looked at me but we never said a word. She opened her blue door, once inside turned to face me and opened her arms. In the safety of her embrace she told me she would always love me. She kissed me as I sobbed and told me it was necessary for me to go back to the main house; perhaps my mother needed me.

She assured me in the morning we would have tea but somehow this prospect did not have the desired effect. The walk back to the main house stayed with me like the tattoo on my ass does now. Thinking about these things brought back tears. I felt sad but not desperate, as I once did. I hated myself then for being incapable of changing anything at all. Late at night after everyone was in bed, I sat on own my bed holding the two square pillows

Maman had embroidered, one with a butterfly and the other with *Je t'aime*. I could not cry and was numb except for a gut-wrenching feeling. So many years have passed since that day; I never forgot that pain.

Memories are all I have. When I woke up from the evening of hell, still holding the pillow with the butterfly, I decided to seek understanding with Suzannah. I showered and dressed quickly and with my hair still wet, I ran to her house. In my arms was the pillow embroidered with Je t'aime. My hope for waking up from a nightmare did not materialize. She had boxes neatly stacked in one corner of her living space. She smiled when I barged in.

"I have a great tea for you to try this morning."

I gave her the pillow and I watched her as she placed it with great care inside a box that was still open. I asked her how she could be so calm and where did she get the boxes? The night before they were not in her living room. I also wanted to know where she would go.

She held me only for a moment. "Julienne, sometimes the fight is taken out of you and sometimes you must be prepared. I must ready myself to depart as soon as I can arrange for the transportation of my belongings. I am happy I am not a collector."

She asked me if I remembered her friend Hilda and then told me she would join Hilda and live in the Dominican Republic. She also told me, when they had visited years ago, they had discussed the possibility if one day it became necessary.

"You, my sweet one, have this hour in which to shine and grow in whatever direction you choose. I know the pain you feel and I also know you will make your own happiness. No matter how difficult life is, ultimately we choose life or we choose to let go. It is better for your mother to put distance between us. I will know great sadness and so will you, but we will be fine. I know it. I will let you know the new address because I think Hilda's place is too small for both of us. But here, I have the present address for you. Write and visit me when the time is right. You will know when that is. It is the hope of seeing you again that will carry me."

She held me tighter as I sobbed.

"I am grateful we had almost twenty-four years to know and love one another. Not everyone under similar circumstances can have such experiences. I am thankful to your father; he was a miracle worker, a man of honor. I will always be with you even if we live oceans apart." She released me and told me to drink my tea.

"I added some ginger roots and also cinnamon in the tea. I remembered you liked it very much the last time I made tea with those ingredients."

I felt a tear rolling down my cheek as I got up and decided to boil water while I looked for my cinnamon, black tea and ginger. In New England, it was a Saturday morning.

The Canvas

The last time I saw Suzannah, she blew me a kiss, brought her left hand up and her index finger to her mouth, indicating no other words were necessary. Her right hand was on her heart. Both my hands over my heart as tears freely flowed. A taxi had been waiting. It was done. My life, once more, had been jolted and changed.

And Paul Deschamps

I must have thought the pain I felt would vanish if I called Paul. I wanted someone to make it all go away and he could. As usual, he sounded delighted to hear from me during my moment of despair. He suggested I come to his apartment. Drinking and making love would make me feel better. Before the end of our conversation I knew, this time I wanted to stay with him. The knowledge of how irresponsible an action this was no longer caused me anguish. Maman was sleeping, for that I was happy, and after my call to Paul I wrote her a note letting her know I would be visiting a friend for several days. She still did not know Paul or anything about him. I packed a red nightgown, a silk camisole, my American jeans, three blouses, if one could really call them blouses, two evening dresses and shoes. My little suitcase was bulging. I left the note on the dining room table and got into my Renault. Paul had been my lover long enough to know how we would be spending our days or nights together. He was not working for the moment but I had the means to support our time together. My mood changed and off I went to the arms of my lover, hoping that all would be right with my world and me. With a glass of wine he greeted me. Although it was early in the morning, we drank and made love and then he suggested we get married. The angels were singing! Right then we decided to drive to Monaco, spend the night and marry the following day. With a fait accompli, mother would have to accept him.

The drive was grand, filled with anticipation and laughter. Paul looked better than ever before. We arrived early enough to see the sun set. He suggested we get married before dinner, and I agreed.

Dressed not like a bride, we went to the Prefecture where an agent in a gray suit married us. I purchased two wonderful wedding bands for us to wear. Back in our room, as Mr. and Mrs. Deschamps, we again made love. After a while, we dressed and went back to the casino where he played a lot and lost a lot. I walked the corridor away from the casino, the thought of something wrong exploded inside my head. I was very foolish then and I am glad life has seasoned me enough to recognize the Paul Deschamps of this world.

While he gambled my money away, I looked at display windows, entered boutiques, well adorned with clothes and jewelry awaiting the next winner. I was bored and decided to find the nearest bank. A new sequenced top and my jeans would lure Paul away from the roulette table.

The bank manager recognized me from two or so years ago, when I was there with my mother and father. He walked up to greet me and, almost in the same breath he commented on my beauty and offered his condolences. Conversation was almost impeccable, yet a risqué. I asked him for additional credit. Mr. Rouse escorted me to his office and made a telephone call. I heard, oui, oui, ha, oui, je vois, after which he turned to me and without ceremony told me credit had to be denied. Stunned, I got up without asking for any explanation, I went to find Paul. After our first argument he suggested I call my mother.

"Hello Maman, I am in Monaco, and just got married to Paul Deschamps,"

Before I could say another word, "I know where you are and I suggest you drop your gigolo and return home immediately."

I was in a state of utter panic; Paul did not argue with me when I told him about the conversation with my mother. Instead, he told me he would not stay married to a woman who could not support him. If my mother would not release the funds, she would have to pay a settlement for a divorce. I was devastated. Paul was not in love with me. I was a commodity and nothing more. As I thought about this, I wondered how I could have allowed myself this disaster. More than two years after my father's death, the signs were certainly there, but I had chosen not to see them. I was longing for something and at the time, I did not know lust and love were not the same.

It was during the drive back home that I began to regain my senses. I was almost ready to talk with my mother. I even wondered how Paul would get home.

Suzannah must have seen what would happen if I did not restrain my impulsiveness. Before going to that studio for dinner and dancing, she insisted on a sermon, "Julienne, though I wish you a good time at this dance, please do not go in with the intention of taking a lover. You are not ready and are also very vulnerable. Please understand that a lover is not a cure for what ails you. If there is an emptiness inside you, neither wine or a man's body will fill it."

I repeated this sentence to myself right after Frank's death when I thought a bottle of Southern Comfort he brought from the United States might ease the pain I felt. When my father died, she reminded me I had not yet digested the emotional or physical implications, she said it took at least three or more years.

"You must find your own balance. Healing takes time, be patient with yourself." Suzannah had a way of exercising good sense, something I was in dire need of. These days I have no intention of engulfing myself in a new love. First, I need to heal something inside me and I know I must take the time to do so.Once Suzannah raved about my having this habit of taking on a new lover whenever the world did not deliver to me what I wished. It always made me angry but she was right. She had an analytical mind and mine ran on impulse. Only now I begin to emulate a better form of behavior.

The Canvas

After driving alone and without music I stopped the car under a tree, and took a short walk, something I had never done before.

It was a glorious day when I left the husband who had no use for me. I found the means to look at the road ahead of me. I understood what Suzannah has said not too long before, but this time I had not just taken a lover. I took on a husband because I was angry. I felt lost, and I missed my father and Suzannah. I was scared because I had no goals or aspirations. I was the blank canvas she referred to. The marriage was a serious blunder. I turned around, walked back to my car. With resolve I restarted the engine. I was ready for whatever the consequences would be.

From that point on the drive was focused and I was no longer crying. Every action had become deliberate. Not going too fast or too slow, I drove at an even speed. Something different was going on. I enjoyed the route I took. There were beautiful trees on all sides. I even noticed occasional houses and gardens. Something had shifted and I wished I could have shared this discovery with Suzannah. Unfortunately, with this shift I also knew wishful thinking would no longer be part of my life.

Mother was not smoking when I arrived very late that evening. She was wearing a beautiful yellow dress. I was glad to see her in something other than black; her yellow dress with no sleeves showed me how much weight she had lost. She walked toward me and embraced me. I could feel her fingers twirling my loose curls the way Suzannah often did. Her only words to me related to the fact I was fine, safe and at home.

Blank Canvas and Clay

When I arrived home I was hungry. Mother and I ate a simple meal of fruit, cheese and bread outside on the veranda where we could see the stars. Mother appeared pleased. There was an air of resplendence around her. She even looked younger. Maman and I did not look alike. I was the mirror image of my father. Suzannah and also aunt Erika often said so.

"Julienne, you are like this beautiful porcelain dish. I am glad you came back home, I was not sure you would return here to be with me. I thank you."

I could not think of anything to say, where else could I go? "I think of you as a piece of clay about to be made into a magnificent plate like this one. You know a lot happens to clay before it becomes porcelain. Only when the lump of clay takes on the desired shape, is it baked in a kiln at very high temperature. Your journey with Paul Deschamps was your initial firing. A baptism by fire; it takes a few of those to make a person whole."

She was still holding an empty plate in her hand. As usual I had no idea what she was talking about.

"You will come out of it all with brilliance. Be patient. Colors will be applied and I am afraid, back to the oven you will go. This is how life makes us shine. Look at the plate, the graceful rose at its center, the leaves forming a boundary all around as if to protect the delicate flower. So much went into making this a beautiful plate. I chose it for you. I need you to understand that everyone around you loves you, but I wonder if you ever took the time to love yourself?"

For the first time I realized Maman and Suzannah were both concerned about me.

"Dear, while you were sleeping with Paul I had him investigated. I must say I did not think you would marry him. He is a gigolo who has sustained his miserable life by taking from vulnerable rich women. You are not the first and I doubt will you be the last to succumb his charm. I do not understand why you thought you were in love with him. At your age you should have recognized the differences between love and lust. Tomorrow I will call our lawyer and begin the divorce proceedings. Do you think this will be an equitable way to rectify what has happened?"

I was stunned; she knew more than I did. I agreed to rectify what had happened! Suzannah was not there and all I wished for was to be with her. My mother felt like continuing our conversation, there was no escape. We talked about my continued education. The art institute was wonderful but going on to the Sorbonne to take courses in literature and history was of greater importance. I had talked about it for at least three of the last five years. When I told Mother it was her extensive library that gave me a thirst for these subjects, she was surprised. I explained I also wanted to know more about the stories Suzannah had told me. I wanted to do historical research. She was agreeable to my idea but curious to know what I was looking for. Our tête-à-tête took another direction.

"Regardless, I am proud of you, Julienne. Of late, life has not been perfect. One struggles, one learns, one grows, one accepts things as they are. This is what we are both doing right now. I want you better prepared than I was; it is important in life. One day soon we will talk more about these things. For now, I am happy to have you home. Go to bed, dear. Get a good night sleep; we have a lot to handle before noon tomorrow."

She got up and left me, I came to the conclusion Paul Deschamps could not have replaced my father or Suzannah. I, too, got up and walked to my room. Something inside had gotten stronger, I felt sure I would handle this episode and go on to Paris to study. Frank told me, when he saw me walking around at the Librarie Frost, it was my self-assured posture and walk that attracted him. He followed me from a distance and waited till I took some book from a shelf. I was actually sitting when we met, and American classics were on a chair next to me. The transition between France and the USA may have come from this fountain of assurance I cannot see. Who can say?

Today when I entered my bedroom my thoughts moved in another direction. I scanned every corner, my chairs, my bed with its two square pillows and the doll Frank managed to persuade Jennifer to get for me. She told me she had to hunt this doll down.

195

The people of the town helped her and she found it at a store called the Euro Attic. She said everyone in town knew about this doll. They knew about Frank too. The thought of it made me smile though somewhat ridiculous. On the highboy, the candelabra Suzannah had made for me was ready for the next holidays. She gave it to me on my thirteenth birthday. This Menorah found its way to my bedroom at that time and was still with me. One of the arms had gotten bent in the course of my traverse from one ocean to the other. The place of honor it held had not changed; close to my heart.

The time to strike a match and light the helper was tonight. In the morning paper I had read something about Hanukkah. Eight perfect Aegean blue candles made by Suzannah's hands had withstood a long time. I lit the center candle and did not know what else to do. Watching the flame and knowing Jews used an oil lamp for eight days instead of one, I promised myself and perhaps Suzannah as well, I would learn more about the candle and oil-burning story. That night I slept well.

I awoke with a smile and concluded it would not take me an eternity to embrace the next phase of my life. All the people no longer in my life had given me the tools I needed. Another day had gone by, that night, I walked to my room and at sunset picked up a lighter I kept close to another candle, and once again lit the center candle. I decided to not use the precious candles. I stared a long while, thinking about the many things that were no longer a part of my life. I blew out the candle and watched as a thin stream of gray smoke disappeared but filled the room with the essence of Suzannah. She may not have known the words to say. She did not have to teach them to me, the stillness around me was sufficient. I remembered her and the stories she told.

The High Cost of Impulse

The floodgates had opened. I had returned home safely. The rest would follow. Talking to my mother changed many things. I walked out of my room dressed conventionally in a black skirt, the only one I had, and a white blouse, with two buttons on each cuff like the ones Suzannah wore. I walked to the dining room. Maman had already called the lawyer and we were to meet him in two hours. It was eight in the morning. I saw my mother's subtle smile; her hair had some white strands I had not noticed before. I felt a momentary twinge of guilt for not paying closer attention to her. Our mood was light and my guilt did not last. I sat opposite her and she started the conversation.

"It has been a long time since we had breakfast together. I no longer know what you like. Fruit? A brioche? Do you prefer coffee instead of tea? You have been so engaged in your life and I in my grief I have not paid enough attention to you. Please forgive me, Julienne."

I got up, not taking my eyes away from her gaze, and gave her an expansive hug. I could not remember the last time we hugged and this one solidified something between us. We both had damp eyes but unlike myself, Maman was not inclined to cry or make a scene, not even for me.

The ride to the lawyer was the most fun I had had in my yellow Renault. For the first time my Maman was riding with me. She did not drive and I trust never would after that day. We arrived at the lawyer's about ten minutes before the appointed time. The secretary greeted us and told us she had been able to acquire the necessary information and that the certified copy of the marriage certificate would be mailed to the office in triplicate. In my haste to leave Monaco, I did not think to get the actual certificate we were given. The secretary was a middle-aged woman evidently good at what she did. The lawyer entered the room, his gray suit had a shine to it but it did nothing to elevate his diminutive status. He extended his hand to mother.

"I am Albert Ribonet and I will be handling your divorce." Looking at me was his manner of introduction. What he lacked in height he made up for in confidence. He turned to face my mother and explained the laws of Monaco would prevail since this was where the marriage had taken place. A lawyer from the municipality would handle the various aspects of the divorce, as required by law.

As he explained everything to us, I could not help but remind him we had been married less than 48 hours. I wanted the marriage annulled without going through a divorce and perhaps more. He smiled, and politely explained the work of a gigolo and the fact that all along my husband's intention had been to negotiate the terms of a divorce settlement.

I could not believe my ears. "We were married less than two days, what is there to negotiate?"

With a sly smile, he reminded me again, my husband was a professional who would grant the divorce for a fee. Today I know a bond with my mother was born out of this and could never have occurred otherwise. So many things had happened since that day.

It was almost time to go to the school where Mr. Rand would introduce me to the French Class. I knew all would be well. After the preparations and suggestions this kind teacher had made I was ready to meet this class. According to plans I was to enter the room introduce myself in French and not speak a word of English until the bell rang.

I enjoyed the afternoon with anxious students. They were polite and asked if I could return. Mr. Rand smiled and gave his approval. As I was about to leave the classroom he suggested since I was to come back to his classroom he wanted to talk more about what that session would be like? He also wondered if I would accept an invitation to see a film of French impressionist work that was showing on Main Street. He understood my cordial excuse. A nice man that Mr. Rand I thought...

Nature's Storm

I awoke to pounding sounds around me; through the uncovered window I could see the branches of the trees swaying back and forth. This was a punishable storm I was not quite prepared for. Nor could I tell where the wind and the rain mixed with hail was coming from. Every bit of energy released by this angry weather seemed aimed at my windows. I was afraid the roof would collapse or window glass would shatter. I dressed myself, just in case. It was autumn and I did not know such storms touched this New England harbor. Frank never told me.

Out of my closet I pulled a skirt the color of bark neither green nor brown. The cloth was wool, appropriate for this time. This morning's weather suggested I needed warmth. It was a stylish skirt, not unlike those Suzannah wore. I noticed with a degree of pleasure that quite often that I wore clothes similar to hers, but the blouses I wore had lace or ruffles, and sometimes both. Today's blouse was pale yellow silk with a ruffled neckline. Suzannah's blouses never failed to be white and tailored.

The plan was to visit a new acquaintance but in view of the weather, I felt it was prudent to cancel.

"Be prepared and know you do not control any outcome; just do the best you can." Often I heard this from her so I prepared myself in case the weather did not change. I put my hair up. Frank would call me his jungle bunny when my hair would begin to curl out of control. Rain and humidity played havoc with my curls. I still missed all the fun I had around this loving, beautiful man. He was able to take any life situation and turn it into something worth exploring. Through some miracle, I was neither overwhelmed nor frightened; I had discovered the Yellow Pages; this telephone book could get me to the moon and back. As the rain abated I decided I would handle matters related to home heating. It was getting cold and I had no idea what to do with a furnace. Before his departure, James did not tell me how to make this beast work. We were not thinking of such a change of weather. I went down to the basement to explore and investigate. Better lighting for this enormous room was evident. Going back to the Yellow Pages, I looked for advertisements and then I wrote down some names and numbers. At the end of the porch, my firewood had gotten wet and perhaps unusable. Tea, black and strong, was needed and while the water boiled it occurred to me that my entire life I had taken everything for granted. The workings of the world around me had been transparent enough but I never noticed. *Be prepared* came back to mind, but then so did *do your best.*

Paper, pen and telephone became my friends. While waiting for the service man, I found the very beautiful multi-colored shawl Frank had given me. I am sure he had such a day in mind. I wrapped it around my neck. In America I discovered service people took their time to appear for a job. James did not keep me waiting an entire day when I needed him. I hoped they were having a wonderful time in Bermuda.

Another unopened box demanded my attention and rather than wait aimlessly for the serviceman I went to the guest bedroom to tackle its content. Another thought took center stage.

Mother and also my father were vacationing, and Suzannah and I were to meet them in Morocco. According to my parents, it was a convenient place to go, and the reason for this, I knew nothing about. To me a vacation was anywhere I could explore and have fun. My mind continued to travel from one place to the next as the chill in the house became unbearable. The heat from the fireplace was not sufficient to warm the entire house. I moved to the library; some logs in that fireplace were waiting for me to strike a match. The flames were amber with some blue, a good sign. Dreaming about warm places was better in warm rooms. It was not yet my birthday but Suzannah gave me a present. A ring, the stone was a Citrine and I had never heard of it. She told me it was the gemstone exhibiting success, power and intelligence. On either side of the stone were two very small diamonds. I felt as if I had just become engaged but there was no prince on his knees putting a ring on my finger. We were in the backyard of a sprawling house with two fountains in the front and at least twenty-five steps to the front door. I smiled a moment thinking of my seven steps. The gardens were well manicured but nothing like my mother's. The ground had enormous gray stones to walk on and the scent exploding from two tall trees with white flowers was intoxicating. We were told the trees came from China. Why trees from China would make it to Morocco, I will never know. As I thought about such things, I become increasingly aware of life's chaotic ambiguities. They were all around me. No one seemed to have known the names of these trees, just as I still did not know the names of all the trees surrounding my property nor where they came from. This may not have mattered a great deal but it was sad to be surrounded by so many unknowns. I resolved to do something about the trees in my own yard. In Morocco, my mother and father joined us and soon informed Suzannah they would be gone again, a while. Before leaving us, my father pulled some Durham out of his pocket. The currency of Morocco was given to Suzannah because I was not trusted with money. With a new ring on my finger I never asked where they were going. It did not matter to me.

We rode a camel most days but walking was my preference. I could check things out and I could touch them. We were where Muslims and Jews and Christians did business. We were told many times all three religions were born out of Jerusalem, which did not make sense to me. I had other concerns; the money was yet intact in Suzannah's care.

We came across a narrow path complete with a few goats munching on papers and even some rags. A donkey with baskets on his back passed us. He must have known where he was going because he was travelling alone. I smiled because I was also traveling life alone. The donkey may have known where he was going but only now I was finding my own path ——This zigzagging path led to stairs and more alleys; one took us toward a village where the houses were made of mud. They were white washed and looked like sculptures. A rounded door within a larger arch revealed a word we understood: Restaurant. We were greeted with a particular glow from the sunrays. The interior walls covered with hand-woven fabrics were colored mostly ochre red and blue. The embracing hues warmed us to the bones. Suzannah pointed to a yellow hand woven wall hanging. She mentioned it was almost the color as the star the Jews wore during the war. An old man approached us; he must have been a hundred, very thin with a long white beard and not a hair on his head. He spoke Hebrew, I think; Suzannah indicated she did not understand. He then spoke German to her. He showed me his right arm. He too had a number tattooed on it. Seconds later his wife, I presumed, invited us to her shop. She was the weaver. The gentleman went on toward a galleria. He was working with dyes, cottons and wools used to make magnificent tapestries. My mother's prized Gobelin tapestry came to mind. I did not like it when I was young and now it is in my dining room. A lady with a simple blue djellaba brought our food. We had not ordered anything but were told the man and his wife had taken the liberty of ordering for us. I am not sure how long I daydreamed about Morocco. The weather changed and the sky opened to an awesome and inspiring rainbow. I heard the gate and the repairman made his way to the driveway. My last piece of wood had done its job in the library while the rest of the house was colder. The man drove his little green truck and stopped by the steps. He got out of his truck with caution and I noticed he had only one leg and he had no difficulties climbing my seven steps.

He told me my heating unit was new, and he adjusted a few things and told me to set the thermostat where I felt comfortable. I was not yet accustomed to Fahrenheit. He set the temperature at 69 degrees and told me to bring it up if that felt too cold.

He did not charge me because he said he did nothing. He walked down the steps and told me to recommend him to my friends.

A New Store to Explore

It was a brisk Saturday morning when I entered the little coffee shop. Sarah's something was the name, and my intention was to buy some interesting pastries. I missed good pastries and so far, for my taste, the American ones were too sweet.

Two young girls, standing by the counter, were giggling and talking about the ball. There was so much excitement in their voices. Looking about, I saw no ball and in my effort to find new friends of any age, I decided to ask about it. Age did not matter to me, so I introduced myself, told them I was new in the USA and wanted to explore everything American. I wanted to know about this invisible ball. The taller of the two said she was Amy, and the other, Linda. They explained to me, they were sixteen and tonight was their sweet-sixteen party. They asked if I had any sons and if so, did they speak English. I gathered they had detected my accent. After getting this important question out of the way, they asked me where I was born. Once I answered and also informed them I had no sons, they were satisfied. With no sons of mine to dance with, they left the store. The interest in my place of birth left with them.

Still browsing the isles, I found a collection of interesting cups and decided one of them would be wonderful for my morning tea. The display of fine porcelain and other items was exquisite. I heard a voice asking if I wanted to purchase the cup and saucer I was holding. I turned and the lady I had not noticed before caught my breath. I very nearly fainted. I was looking at the ghost of Suzannah. She was older, but the hair, the body, the height and face, all were Suzannah's. I put the saucer and cup on the counter. I could not answer because no words came out. She approached me and this time asked if I was all right. I detected a slight German accent. She pulled out a chair and asked me to sit down; I did, like a rag doll.

It took a long while for me to compose myself and then I asked: "Do you have a sister named Suzannah?" This time the tables were turned. She became rigid, her eyes staring at me with the same penetration Suzannah's eyes could express. Suddenly, she lowered her eyes perhaps because she did not want me to notice a certain swelling. She looked around. We were alone in the store and I could not move. She pulled a chair up next to mine and she asked, "How do you know Suzannah?"

Several hours passed before I ended my story about how I knew Suzannah. She took my hands.

"I am Ursula but many years ago I changed my name to Sarah in an effort to erase the memories of a day I still cannot forget."

I told her I was Julienne Fairchild. A young couple entered the store and our conversation ended. I told her I would return to buy the cup in a day or two. Three other couples walked in. I gathered it was time for Saturday morning coffee with friends at Sarah's Coffee Shop. One day my intention is to become one of the patrons, but first I had to know more about Ursula, or Sarah, as she called herself.

The drive back home was almost surreal. Suzannah never told me about a sister named Ursula or Sarah. I drove feeling as I had the first time I was on these roads. Something unsettling yet exciting was happening. I decided to make a gargantuan effort not to think about what had happened earlier. Instead, I would think of the girls and their sweet-sixteen party.

"Happy Birthday, Julienne, I just finished an embroidered handkerchief for you. I am not very good at this sort of thing but I know you will like it. Tonight when you are dancing and twirling away, you may need it. I bet there will be pearl size beads of sweat pouring down your face. Make sure you enjoy every minute. It is not every day one is sixteen. Laugh at the funny jokes and fall in love at least three times during the night. I am so happy for you. I did not have a party or go anywhere on my sixteenth birthday. Do you want me to wash your hair and give you a beautiful hairdo? I can do it if your mother allows it."

As always my mother allowed it. She had a hard time with my head full of curls although as I got older my hair became less curly.

"I can almost see you dancing and having fun. This is a day you will remember always. Please keep in mind I want to know all about it tomorrow. "

Suzannah was the one who taught me everything I knew about geography, geometry, mathematics and piano. Italian and dancing, too, she also taught me. But she never told me about having any relative. Who was this woman? I was driving when a heavy downpour began and with each drop on my windshield, my mind summoned memories of the day I became sixteen.

That day Suzannah came into my bedroom to help me with at least fifty buttons on the back of my pale yellow dress. It was almost like a bridal gown with pearl buttons but no train. Its full skirt was made for dancing. Suzannah started brushing my long dark curly hair, pulling the sides up to the middle of my head and allowing a cascade of shiny curls down my back. The entire hairdo was held in place by a barrette covered with pearls. The barrette also exposed small yellow and white ribbons going down the side of my head. I never looked so beautiful. She took a few steps back.

"Tonight your canvas will be painted with primary colors, I can see it, brilliant! Reds and yellows, and blues, all primary colors, all vibrant."

Mother came into my bedroom she was visibly taken. I was standing like a princess, my crown of ribbons exposing my shinny curls. She thanked Suzannah, as a way of dismissing her.

For a moment I felt sad, again I noted she tolerated but did not like Suzannah.

Mother told me to behave like a lady and not perspire! How interesting this scene was. The two most important women in my life wished me two different and distinct outcomes at this ball.

When my driveway became visible, I made my turn and drove to the new garage in the back of the house. I had no pastries with me. The small veranda was also an addition to my home, and it had become another place to daydream. I sat a moment. I needed to pause. In this veranda I had only one chair and one table, they were both white and pants guaranteed to flower were in blue and white planters from Italy. I sat a long while, imagining the pond not yet built.

I went empty-handed to the kitchen and answered the telephone when it rang.

The Telephone Call

At the other end I recognized the soft accented voice.

"Mrs. Fairchild, this is Ursula. Your house is on my way home and I was hoping it would be all right for me to drop by?"

My hands shook and got sweaty. "Yes, of course you may stop by. I will put some water on; we can have some tea."

There were no other words, just a click. I looked everywhere in the kitchen for what I could offer her. I had a few petit-beurre left, a little stale perhaps but I had nothing else; they would do. I could offer her a glass of wine, some cheese and crackers, but I had no crackers, and no bread. After my encounter with Ursula, I did not stop anywhere to buy the things I had gone out to get. I stopped fretting and took a deep long breath, the way Suzannah had instructed me to do. I heard the car's door. Ursula did not have suitcases to carry up my stairs; she made it to the front door with a small box. Without ceremony, she handed it to me.

"I took the liberty of bringing you some pastries. This morning I wanted to talk more with you, but, as you know, it was not possible. Thank you for giving me your name. You made my search easy. So here I am. I was going to bring you the cup and saucer you admired this morning but I broke the saucer. I was so nervous; I will order another one for you."

215

A surge of compassion enveloped me. I took her hand, as Suzannah had so often taken mine. I escorted her to my reading room where, for the first time, the two blue plaid chairs would be used. Four days before I had two pictures framed. One with Frank angled in a bookcase so I could see it when in my chair. The other picture was with Suzannah. I had I it in the other bookcase facing the door. I could see her when I came into the room. She stopped in front of the second picture. Suzannah was a self-assured woman; Ursula felt less so. Standing in front of the picture I noticed the resemblance.

She took that picture and held it to her heart, as she sat in the chair facing the window, eyes visibly wet. Not knowing what to say, I suggested I make some tea because I wanted to taste one of her pastries. She followed me to the kitchen still holding the picture to her heart and sat by my little table.

"Did Suzannah ever tell you about me?"

I had to tell her the truth and felt troubled by my admission. "No, Suzannah did not talk much about her family. We were close but there were things she never talked about. Maybe you can tell me more."

"It is such a long and horrible story. I never talk about horrible things although they are too impossible to forget. I can tell you Suzannah was my younger sister. Our parents were both killed in Germany because they were Jews. We were hiding in a cave-like

216

place my father excavated behind the kitchen and covered with dirt, hay and other things. We heard the soldiers shoot my father when he asked them to leave his property. This request cost him his life. The life of a Jew was without value. We waited a long while; I think this is when Suzannah fell asleep. There was not a sound and mother decided to investigate. I think, hearing our mother scream after more shots were fired and knowing they had shot our father, was too much for Suzannah. She cried for hours and after a while I went out to look around. I am no longer sure when Suzannah fell asleep but I left her with the intention of coming back. I broke the comb mother had given me and gave half of it to her, just in case, I guess. I was hoping to find my parents, hurt, perhaps, but still alive. I did not know there were a few SS left behind. I was captured, raped and later taken to a train station. It was a packed train. I do not know where it was going. There was no water or food for anyone, and we were packed in like sardines. I was bleeding a great deal because one soldier used his gun to rape me with. One woman took a piece of fabric she was carrying for some reason and put it between my legs. She told me to press it against me. There was no place to sit, so I stood and I suppose after a while, the bleeding stopped. I do not know if I fainted but while the train was moving slowly, a wooden slat broke. There was just enough space for me to slip through, and I jumped. I rolled round and round but no one saw me. To my knowledge, no one else jumped. When I finally came to a stop, the train had gained speed and was gone. I stayed there a

217

while, not knowing where to go or what to do. I did not even know where I was. I stayed in the woods for many days. I have no idea how I survived. A very decent German woman and her sister rescued me. They were not Jews, just good people. I spent the war years hidden mostly in their attic or their basement, next to some potatoes. When the Allied armies came, again I was rescued. First I was taken to Texas where a Jewish group sponsored me and then I came here. This is when I changed my first name to Sarah, and the Weiss family gave me their last name by adopting me when I arrived in the USA. So Muller was no more, but the memories did not vanish with a change of name or country. I have been here in Maine all this time. I did not know where Suzannah was or if she was alive. I did not know how to find her. So finally I had to give up. I became a nurse and worked at the local hospital. About five years ago, after I retired, the store where you came became available so I bought it."

As tears rolled down her face, it occurred to me that she cried much like Suzannah, making not a sound. She missed her family and her sister she said many times. Then she showed me a piece of a comb and said this was the only physical thing she had as a reminder from a time when she had a family. She asked me questions about Suzannah. She wanted to know if she was tall and slender or was she heavy, her hair color and so on. She never asked me how I had come to know Suzannah. But maybe we could talk another time. Perhaps we could become friends; we could be like family. I felt a great deal of compassion for her. It was after eleven o'clock when she left and since she arrived at six twenty, she looked spent. I thanked her, hugged her and told her I would like to see her again. She took the stairs one slow step at a time. Her gait was now labored and she showed her age and the trauma of her life. After her car made it out of the driveway, I went back inside and put the picture back in place. We had not touched the pastries. This was not an evening for sweets.

Looking for Frank's embrace, I continued to wonder why Suzannah never told me she had a sister.

The Box

I looked for pictures I could share with Sarah, wondering all the while if I should call her Ursula. I needed to know more about her. None of the information I had or stories I had heard included a lost sister. Why did Suzannah not tell me? I did not need a blood test to know they were sisters. Not twins, but sisters for certain. I gathered a few good pictures of Suzannah, some of my parents, and one of Frank. In memoriam, I placed the packet of photos in a large envelope to be delivered to Sarah the next day. I was outside the door before the store opened with envelope in hand. It was just about 9:00 AM. I wanted to know more about Sarah and I hoped we could talk between customers. Soon after my arrival at the store, I realized she was getting emotionally drained. I told her I needed to make another stop, gave her the envelop and left. There was so much I wanted to know but it was not yet the right time. I stopped and got the groceries I had needed to buy the day before. The drive home was uneventful and so I thought about the box Suzannah had left for me. Hilda had given it to me when I went back to the Dominican Republic with the intention of convincing Suzannah to come back home with me. I think, like me, her heart had been broken. Her reason to stay alive was no longer important, with no hope and no will she could not survive. It was impossible to know if it was shame or guilt that kept me from opening the box. I made one more stop before reaching my driveway. I walked along the beach until I was too tired to think.

The sound of rain woke me up. I had become accustomed to heavy rain alternating with periods of sunshine, but overall, the weather was getting colder every day. My bedding included a blanket and the down filled comforter I purchased the first day I went on a tour of Paris with Frank.

Suddenly, I could feel Frank kissing my neck as he pointed to a bronze dancer in a window. I no longer remember the dancer in detail. It stayed at the store, to be sold to someone else. I only know how I felt after the kiss. The feeling stayed with me and that night I danced for him and soon after his bed needed no covers to keep me warm. Here alone I used what once was unnecessary.

After dressing I went into the guest bedroom and retrieved Frank's fisherman sweater. I had grown to love it. Still too long and too big for me since washing it did not result in shrinking it. I felt I needed it. I was going to open the box Suzannah left for me. My chairs were waiting for me, one on each side of the table with the Tiffany lamp. I chose the one closest to the window. Today the beautiful wood box Suzannah left me was next to the pictures. Sarah had put it there instead of back on the mantle. While examining it, she told me her father used to carve boxes and Suzannah loved to watch him.

The rain continued relentlessly. The garden was wet and each leaf was washed clean. In my room innumerable fragrances assaulted my senses. I made myself a cup of tea, feeling alive and free of fears.

No fanfare, no flowers from Frank but from Suzannah, the box. I had had this box in my possession since 1973 and today on my birthday November 14, 1980 I was finally going to open it. A seven-year cycle must have a special meaning. In any case, it was a very long time to be afraid to open a box. Suzannah's sister must have had the secret key. The humidity in the air allowed the wood's aroma to permeate my nostrils, if not the entire room. It was not cedar but must have been an exotic wood from the Dominican Republic; it had the scents of the great outdoors.

In my black wool skirt I was ready for the inclement weather; the long sleeved blouse, and Frank's fisherman's sweater orchestrated the mood. For the first time, I was anticipating the contents of the box with a sense of relief. All fears I had took a holiday. My old teacup and saucer were on the table ready for the periodic pauses. It had not been a matter of exercising patience that kept me from opening the box. It was a matter of fear of the unknown. Today none of my past feelings were present. Whatever had stopped me before had vanished.

I picked up the box from the shelf. It seemed lighter than the last time I had dusted it. The subtle aroma from the wood was pleasing and in an odd way the feeling was better than moments before. I was examining the workmanship. Every stroke of the artist's knife could be experienced. Vines grew out of the wood veins to form a paisley pattern around the box. On each side there was a peacock, much like the ones on the pillows Suzannah had. The design itself bore her personal stamp. I could find no signature on the bottom of the box. The top was also carved and formed a slightly rounded cover. The paisley design returned toward the vine. The intricate design continued toward the silver latch. The work was exquisite. In a single line, the design changed again into something resembling the shape of my tattoo. It was incrusted with miniscule red opaque stones I did not recognize. The same red tone was on my ass. How Suzannah remembered the shape of a tattoo I showed her for only a few seconds was incomprehensible. I was certain she had influenced every detail of the carving. The artist did an incredible job translating her words. He could not have known the shape of my tattoo or the embroidered peacocks on the cushions she had in her living room. I could not help but think it would not have been unlike Suzannah to take up carving just to do this work. My fingers caressed the wood, speculating about such possibilities.

The silver clasp was delicate but tarnished, a visible expression of my poor housekeeping skills. At the very edge of this clasp, what I thought was the artist's signature as not, I read the numbers: 4 3 2 7 5 4.

Suzannah had to carve this box. She would not have given this number to anyone. My feelings of anticipation gave way to tears.

With trembling fingers and tear-filled eyes, I lifted the box and heard nothing when I shook it. Not a sound! Had Suzannah left me an empty box? She had a weird sense of humor and it would be just like her to exasperate me one last time. The joke was on me. It was an empty box much like the blank canvas she accused me of being. Seven years in the offing, I opened the delicate clasp. I wanted to see how the inside of this box was made. The box was not empty

The Letter

Meine Julienne,

This is a long overdue letter. For decades I attempted to tell you what would make its way into this letter. Forgive me; I never knew the right words. I am not sure I know them now. Yet, I must do this; so forgive my failure to act when I was supposed to, forgive me for all the things I kept from you, even on your twenty-first birthday, when I got so close to telling you.

I do not know where to begin. My thoughts may not follow any logic, and I am not sure I remember everything as it happened. As I got older the sequences lost their place. I only know how much I love you, my sweet child. I know I must write this letter. It is the time for that. Right now for no reason other than self-indulgence I would give anything to lay my eyes on you, and enjoy the smile I will never forget. The head full of curls like your father's and your eyes full of mischief. I miss you so much.

Before continuing, I must tell you, I did not abandon you. I had to make some hard choices because of a promise I made. It is so hard when one does not know where to start. I kept my promises and now I must tell you many things.

The telephone rang. For a moment I stopped reading but did not answer. I did not remember my father with a full head of curls. He kept his hair very short. I was puzzled and curious. I took a sip of my cold tea as I returned to the letter.

I guess it is best to tell you some of the events that preceded your life. I was still young when Germany was taking the lives of Jews as part of their 'Final Solution.' A way to control I do not know what. I have my own opinions on that but it does not have to do with my letter to you. History tells a great deal but that too has no bearing on this letter.

One afternoon, soldiers came to our farm after my father had moved us from Poland to Germany. As I understand it, a doctor was needed in Rustenburg; it was a good opportunity for him, my mother said. At that time, the situation was difficult for a general practitioner in Poland — especially a Jewish one. My mother always wanted a farm, so this move was good for both of them. I did not understand about Jews in Poland or in Germany, so, the move made no sense to me. I was too young and no one talked to me. Our home was at the edge of town, my father believed we would all be safe. There was a lot of green pasture and beyond that, a wonderful forest where we could pick berries. We were happy, my sister Ursula and me.

I again stopped and this time I got up and filled my cup with some warm tea. So I knew for certain, Ursula and Suzannah were sisters.

I never told you about Ursula, forgive me for that too. It would have been too hard to talk about her, still not knowing if she was alive or dead.

As I write to you, I can remember the noise of the motorcycles, cars and trucks, more noise than you could ever imagine, along with voices of many soldiers. My father was a man with great pride, a sense of justice and fairness. That compelled him to defend his family and his farm, so he ordered the intruders out. Mother, Ursula and I were downstairs; Mother was sewing. I told you Jews had to wear a yellow Star.

Before I was born, my family moved from Austria to Poland. No one told me why. Then we relocated to Germany, but I told you that already. I think my father did not want soldiers bothering him or his family. No one ever told me much about why people moved from one place to the other. Anyway, no one was sick that day to keep him at the clinic so he was home with us. He decided to take me with him when he went out.

I am sorry for rambling. I must write everything I want you to know, chronologically or not. Writing this is difficult and my mind wanders. On that fateful day, first we went to the bank to get some money. That took a long time because of the conversation with the banker. They refused to give my father any of his money. Father was very upset, but there was nothing he could do. He told me times were difficult but we would be all right.

We went to the only small almost empty mercantile store still open. Most of the people in the town had left or simply disappeared. With the money he had in his pocket, my father purchased seeds for my mother's garden, an old book for Ursula who was always reading. I got a special treat, two pieces of hard candy, which the storekeeper had made herself. She had a bag of sugar, she said, and in the store nothing else was sweet. You know I love hard candy and dark chocolate, but the store had no chocolate.

My father told Herr and Mrs. Stubenstein he wanted to do more work on the farm because he felt food rations would continue for a long time and, as it was, everyone was almost starving. He told the shopkeepers about the bank's refusal to give him his money and they discussed what they were going to do. Perhaps talk to the banker again, but they were afraid. We ate a lot of soup in those days and my father said there were almost no vegetables to make soup. The elders talked a while more, and every time someone entered the store everybody saluted. "Heil Hitler!" My father's armband fell and he put it in his pocket. A lady I did not know, who looked three times the size of my father, told him he should have it fixed "Schnell!" She looked menacing, much like a large witch. We left the store and rushed home with some seeds for my mother's garden. I do not know what kind of seeds they were. I carried the old book and one of my pieces of candy for my mother who liked sweets too. Ursula would read aloud for us, she liked that better than candy.

The soldiers arrived soon after we got home. We were all in the kitchen; mother had just made some tea, a mixture of black tea and other leaves she collected in the forest. She did not drink any. She was busy with her sewing kit. My father went out to the front of the house to see what was going on. By the way, his name was Leonard; he had brown almond shaped eyes and light brown hair. Mother always teased him about the size of his nose.

We heard the soldiers shouting at my father. By that time Mother was fixing the armband on the sleeve of his dark suit. The odious armband with its dreaded yellow star with JUDE in the middle was being sewed on the sleeve. The soldiers were outside and we were inside. Mother got up and took us downstairs to the back room. We used it to store things and for my father's medical papers and some medicine. Most of the shelves were empty. There was a green armoire on one wall and it had to be moved. Mother did this without effort, I do not know how. I saw the door and we were pushed in, with Mother right behind us. A special handle allowed her to put the armoire back where it was. I could not hear what was being said, I could tell people were shouting but their words were muffled. Then I heard my father's voice, louder than I ever heard it before. He ordered the men to get out of his property.

I heard more voices, some laughter, then gunshots. More distinctive laughter followed. They were in the house and they broke things. I heard one said something about "gin in the truck" I guess they drank a lot. There was less noise and none from my father. He had no sound left in him.

My mother took us where father had piles of hay. Nothing made sense to me. I wanted my father but knew I could not call out for him. With a swift motion Mother grabbed my arm and shoved me, and my older sister under the hay. She told us not to move, not to cry and not make a sound. She told us when everything had grown totally still we were to move the hay and the bottom plank. The tunnel would take us out. Up to that very day, I did not know we had a tunnel under our house. She said we should walk up the hill toward the mountainside to the right of the house. There were no trails there, not even from any animals I knew about, because I often played there. We heard our mother run in the opposite direction. Meanwhile, Ursula moved something and found a space where we could hide. It was the tunnel, and it was very dark. We stayed at the end of this tunnel for a very long time, not a word spoken and barely breathing. We could not look at each other, I remember that I was shaking.

Mother had said others would be on the opposite side of the mountain to help us. She gave me her ivory comb before running out and she told Ursula who was older with short straight hair, to comb my long hair every day no matter what. Mother also alerted Ursula that under the third tree that we knew for its apples, we would find three liter bottles of water and a leather pouch with money. To find these things we were to take four steps toward the creek but still be under the tree. When my mother kissed each of us on the forehead before she ran out, I could feel her shaking. I can still feel the tremor of her fingers when she touched my shoulder near my neck. Sometimes, I can almost smell her and feel the gentle shaking of her hand.

Mother ran toward the noise, perhaps she went looking for our father. I heard voices again, many voices. Then I heard my mother scream, and then later, I heard her scream again. Then there were no more screaming, just one loud pop. I do not know how much time passed but eventually we heard the voices again — cars, trucks, and motorcycles were all leaving. This loud exit took only minutes but felt like an eternity.

That day the life I had known with my family changed forever. I cried and Ursula kept caressing my head. She never said a word. We understood, and somehow, I escaped into a deep sleep.

When I awakened, it was darker than when we had entered the tunnel. Ursula was not there. I heard a strange noise. I waited but Ursula did not return. I remember my silent tears dropping on the front of my dark blue dress. I cried without a sound because I remembered Mother had warned me to be silent. The strange noise got louder and then I smelled the smoke. I found the comb in my hand but it had been broken. Only a half of it was in my hand. When I crawled out of the pile of hay, I put the comb in my pocket. Ursula had not combed my hair and somehow instinctively I knew she would not return.

I walked toward the third tree; it was a lot further away than I remembered. I hoped Ursula would be there waiting for me so that I would not need to be afraid anymore. It was a very dark night and Ursula was nowhere to be found. I knew where the water and the money were, but in the dark, I was not sure of anything. Fear overwhelmed me but I did not make a sound. I remember my body shaking. This was a fear I would experience again and again.

Both my parents had been killed — I knew that — but I did not know what had happened to my sister. I was thirsty, hungry and like my mother I was shaking. Behind me, all I could see were the flames burning our home and everything I held dear. I walked toward the tree, with darkness in front of me, and flames behind me. I was tired, and afraid but I knew I had to find that tree. It took longer than I thought to get there and I tried to imagine where I would find the water. I circled the tree, once, then one step farther out and circled it again. I did this four times until at last my right foot found the crevice. And there, at my feet, was the treasure I sought. I sat and cried for a long time. My tears did not change what had happened. I was alone. I drank some water and it did not make me feel any better.

After the worst night imaginable to a child, I knew I had to start walking. I walked perhaps six days. Sometimes I fell but I understood that I had to get far away from our farm. I occupied my mind with the stories Ursula used to tell. Thinking of her made me stronger. After a long while, I was less frightened. Somehow, I found the determination and strength to walk. When I was thirsty, I drank some water, but I made sure I did not drink too much even though the bottles were heavy. I had put the money pouch in my pocket. I found berries and ate them and kept walking. At night I rested and slept under trees but I was cold all the time. After many days of walking, the sun came up and I saw an old woman dressed like a farmer, wearing a gray dress and a flowered babushka on her head. She gestured for me to come to her. I did because I knew I could not walk another day and nothing mattered anyway. I had eaten a few berries, all my water was gone, my shoes had holes, my feet were hurting, and I was cold and scared. The farmwoman took me in a buggy to a place that was different from anything I had ever seen. I was given food, and a cot in the corner of the large whitewashed kitchen. The old woman gave me a bath with warm water. She made a dress for me out of some old clothes she had. I had no clothes except my dirty, torn dress. New warm clothing brought some reassurance and hope. But I had lost my family and there was no reason to be alive, and yet I was. The woman repaired my shoes using thick layers of paper and cardboard to conceal the holes. She returned the half-comb and the pouch to me. I missed my father a lot, and every day when I combed my hair with the half-comb I cried for my mother and my sister. To this day, I do not know if my mother was taken away that dreadful night, or killed on the spot. I still miss my sister and I never found out what happened to her.

Julienne, I am sorry for rambling. It is difficult to share these painful memories yet I know I must because it is time.

I stayed in that old woman's farmhouse for a very long time. There were other kids there and we had things to do around the farm. We had food to eat — most of the time it was soups — and we slept upstairs in a small attic without windows. After a while, some of us were taken to another safe place. No one ever told us where we would be taken. A very nice Austrian woman told us it was better that way. If we did not know, no one else would. If we did not know the names of people, no one else would. Today, I feel sad because I never had an opportunity to thank those who saw to it that I would stay alive. We called the old farmhouse woman Frau Mutter.

Life was complicated and dangerous for all. One day, with two other girls, I was captured. We were on the way to another safe house. The man we called uncle was taking us in his cart. We felt safe but we were wrong. Out of the woods came a battalion of soldiers. A huge man with a stick and a starched gray green uniform took me with him. His chest was as broad as his shoulders were. He had some medals dangling on one side of his shirt. He took me to a makeshift room no bigger than the outhouse we used at the farm. Uncle was shot on the spot. They called him a traitor. One of the girls ran and she too was shot. Leah stood immobile and was also taken by a man.

Another man, a huge man, ripped my dress, while holding me with his body against a table. He had taken me to the kitchen, pulling my hair while he ran his hand up and down my legs. I screamed as loud as I could. The sound of my mother's voice returned to me. Again and again I screamed, then I too fell silent. This man raped me. Two of his friends came in and one after the other they too raped me. They covered my mouth with their huge grotesque hands. One almost choked me with his tongue. My clothes were torn, and because of my screams, they slapped me repeatedly. I had blood on my face and it was very swollen. I threw up and wished I would die but I kept on breathing. No one heard my muffled screams. After a while nothing mattered. A fourth man entered that putrid place. The soldiers buttoned their trousers and left. In less than an hour three different soldiers had raped me. This man was older, possibly the age of my father and he asked me for my age. I did not want to talk to him because I knew what he was going to do. He asked me again and when I told him I was fifteen years old, he apologized for his men and said he had a daughter my age.

We were all taken to a train station several miles away. A kind woman gave me a coat she was wearing. We were desperate, afraid, and tired when the train arrived. We had walked all the way with no water and no food. Only fear motivated us. Whatever would happen next did not matter to me.

Everyone was forced to get on the train, although the car was already filled beyond capacity. We felt like sardines. The little children could not breathe. When the train stopped hours later, each one of us got a tattoo similar to the one I once showed you.

Later that night, the man with the daughter came where we were packed in worse than livestock. He called my name but I did not answer because I was afraid he too would rape me. I wanted to die. He found me, and he took me to a barracks. Then another soldier came to get me but the man with the daughter said I was not a Jew and he would take me to my family. He said he knew them. I was afraid he would make me his slave and rape me because after all, I was a Jew and had never seen him before. I knew, he did not know my family, and I knew what soldiers did to Jewish girls.

I do not know how this man managed. He never told me his name, but I can still see his face. He saved my life. After many train rides, I ended up in a French town and he told me some people would help me there. I was in the South of France; I never knew the name of the first town. Nothing mattered to me, I wanted to die.

Later on, I was taken to Lyon, since I did not speak French, I felt like a cow that would be slaughtered one day for its flesh.

These were difficult times for everyone. A local family took me in, and they gave me clothes and food, and a pair of old shoes. In their house with a clay roof, I stayed in the attic and learned a few words of French. Some people were helpful but others were not.

Julienne, during this time people did things you would not think possible. Humanity has both the capacity for good and also for evil.

This town had a series of Traboules as the people called them. I learned they were the passages hidden above and underground. This was the way we travelled through that town. Everything was very old and smelled musty. I think it might have been a fishing village. I had no mother, no father, and no sister. I was far from home, did not understand the language of this village, and there was no one to talk to about how I felt, but I was still alive. In spite of everything, the survival instinct remains strong but I had very little hope. Perhaps this is when I learned to keep to myself. What happened to me held no significance, because I was already dead? The day I lost my family, part of me died, and the day I was raped the rest of me did at least I thought so but one day that too changed.

240

All I had left from the recent past was a piece of my mother's ivory comb. Did you find it at the bottom of the box?

I worked in a different village next to a port where I learned to clean fish. This town was Cannes. The sand and the water were beautiful, and sometimes we walked the beach, but that was dangerous. We were Jews. Languages must have been easy for me, for I soon understood French. I heard the nun, talking about finding us homes with people outside of the area. There were two dozen girls and things were very difficult. We were given a bunk to sleep in, some clothes and fish soup and vegetables to eat. We slept in an attic. This one had one window, I can tell you the word "luxury" immediately came to mind although we were not allowed to open the window or have any lights on. I am not sure where the boys slept. In that attic I found an old apron. It became precious to me because my mother had one. It is the little things that can make a difference in one's life. For me at this time, it was the apron. It had a large pocket in front with a middle seam. I kept my mother's comb on the left side, close to my heart. You may not have any interest in any of this, but I am writing what comes to mind.

Julienne, there is so much I should have told you, but because of pain, and promises I made, I chose not to talk about them. This letter is opening my grief-stricken soul to you. No matter how war affected me, I am grateful for you in my life. I have enormous gratitude to your parents, and your father, who saved my life in many ways.

I was seventeen when a group came to visit the orphanage. It was the third time they had come, with medicines, food, clothes etc, this time, the war had ended but that did not mean anything was normal, whatever normal is. There was a mixture of hope and sadness. I think we each hoped we would reunite with our families. I knew my chances were not good. I did not think my mother and father would have survived being shot, and also the fire. I was no longer afraid to be sad. I did not know how to pray but hoped Ursula would find me. I did not know how to look for her, or where. Among the people visiting the orphanage the Sisters of Mercy operated, there was a nurse who talked to me about letting go of painful memories. I guess she never experienced memories, quite that painful, for they never go away. I do not know how one could simply forget. So much had happened in four years, part of me was still alive but part of me was not. I think no one should meet death as I saw and heard about. Everyday, people around me were dying

By then, I spoke French and Italian well. I sometimes felt guilty because even during moments of despair, laughter was the only relief we had. Funny how that works but laughter helped.

Some of our visitors brought many needed things for the convent. All the girls talked about the handsome and kind men. The women with them who were nurses made sure we were healthy and some took our names and family history. This brought surges of hope to us. They all spoke French among themselves and since I understood I was allowed to spend time with them. Decent good people from the Red Cross, an organization that I had never heard of also visited us. The women wore a white apron with the Red Cross on it. The most handsome man spoke both German and French. We were friends, good friends. He was dressed in a white suit, which was something else I had never seen before. He was not a soldier but a doctor. He brought a lot of food for us, enough so that we were able to prepare a dinner to honor our guests. That evening, the girls wore the nun's uniform given to us when we arrived. We wore this penguin like clothing when outside the convent, even when we went fishing.

I told you this story a long time ago and I hope you remember it. I was cleaning the kitchen, when the handsome man came in. He took my hand and kissed it. I was stunted because no one had ever kissed me gently. I was not afraid of him. He was very tender as he touched my shoulder the way my mother used to but his hand did not shake. His hand was strong yet gentle. He looked at me for what seemed like an eternity. My entire body reacted to his eyes.

He kissed my lips with the gentleness of the afternoon breeze. Afterwards, he apologized for his indiscretion. I heard myself telling him there was no need to apologize. I was smiling and could feel something stirring within me. I had never felt like that before. He took his white coat off, rolled up his shirtsleeves and helped me with the cleaning. When all was spotless, he put his coat back on and asked if we could go for a walk.

Julienne, this imprudence turned into many nights of lovemaking. This man with his gentleness, painted my canvas with a feathered brush. My hope is for you to experience such love, even if only for a moment. Soon my prince had to depart so he kissed my hand again and told me he would return for me. Within a month I knew I was pregnant. Desperate, betrayed and very frightened again, I went to one of the older nuns and told her my situation. This conversation did not go well. I was called many names, none that I thought necessary. I was told I could no longer be around the other girls. I was completely isolated. My new task was to clean the floors and the toilets. I could handle that but I was told when the baby was born it would be given to a deserving couple or put in an orphanage. No family for my child was found. I had a child I could love, I was afraid I would lose her and also knew I could not take care of her needs. I was cleaning Mother Superior's toilet, my little girl was in the basket the cat used, it had been given to me and my baby used it, she was sleeping.

Sister Bernadette said a gentleman was there to see me. This was harder than losing my parents. I thought this person was there to take my baby away. The man looked like Julien, they were brothers he told me. He told me, Julien had been shot days after he left the convent and lived long enough to tell about me. This brother was almost as gentle as Julian and they looked a lot alike. They were twins and most importantly Julian's last wish was that I should be safe, he did not know about my pregnancy.

The twin brother told me his name was Pierre.

I stopped reading, realizing that I was possibly the baby in the cat basket. I was also the baby in the telegram. A surge of emotion overtook me. I knew now why I loved Suzannah as I did. I could not cry. I could only stay still with a feeling of euphoria. Perhaps I even smiled. I took a sip of very cold tea and read more.

He was married but he and his wife had no children. He told me he would like to take me to his home. His wife would be the mother of my child who was four months old by then. I

245

could stay at his home and be safe for the rest of my life. His brother's wish would be respected. There was money to take care of me, and his wife would have the baby she could not bear herself. This would be our secret and I would not be far from my child.

My baby was baptized and adopted and the baby girl was named Julienne. You, Mine Julienne! For so long I dreamed of telling you about our relationship but promises had to be kept. I entertained the idea of telling you after your father died but that would have been a betrayal to him. His wife was still alive and we had an agreement. I left the Mediterranean home your father built for his family and the guesthouse where I lived. I had to respect your mother's request. She had the right to ask that I move out. I did not request to stay, because I knew at that time of her life, she was fragile. You would be in my heart always, and nothing could change that.

In the Dominican Republic I share a small house with Hilda; you met her. (Her husband died) Other Jews reside here as well. Your father, Julien and his group of friends were good to many people here. The Caribbean basin continues to attract Jews. There are still about one thousand left in Cuba. All this is not important. I want you to know, I did not abandon you, my sweet dear child. I learned your mother had passed away when I mailed this letter to you but it was returned to me. I contacted the Proiviens and the Morisseau... Correspondence takes such a long time, but both Mme. Proivien and Mme Morisseau told me about her death and that you had sold the house and moved to Paris. Since then, they had not heard from you. They also informed me Mr. Armand who ran into you in Paris said you were fine and newly married to a fine American but he did not remember the name. I knew the time to tell you this story had come and I missed the opportunity, as I did not know where you were. Mme. Proivien also told me your mother mentioning to her you had married an American. She did not know your new surname either. I must say I chuckled when I thought of your husband and your tattoo. I do not know much about Americans, are they prude? I am sure the man you married must be a great man, one with a sense of humor, I hope. Is he older than you? Did he laugh when he saw your tattoo for the first time? What did you name your children? I know nothing at all about any of this. How I wish I could just reach out and touch your face now.

There is so much I want to tell you, dear child. I want to hold you in my arms as I hold you in my thoughts. I know writing volumes will not serve you or myself but instead, I leave you with the half of my mother's ivory comb. The half I have guarded all these years. Most of all I hope one day this letter will find you.

My time is coming to an end and my body no longer wishes to fight. My heart aches for you, for my parents, my sister, and so much more. I have no choice but to use this letter to tell my heartfelt story.

I thought of creating a map for you. I was going to call it Dreamland but writing this letter was not a dream. I remember how you made me laugh with your escapades when I was trying to teach you geometry. Your mind traveled to Dreamland. Do you remember that?

I am glad I was given the opportunity to be near you as you grew up and I feel so much gratitude because your father could have left me behind. Your father was a good man who honored his brother, and sadly, you will never know how many people he saved. For sure I was one.

Please, Julienne, forgive me for using this method to tell you I am the one who gave birth to you. Now you know my story and you know where your name Julienne came from. I will depart from this life knowing I did what was best for you. I hope one day when you read this letter you will find it in your heart to forgive me. I hope that the ivory comb my mother gave me, although only a half of a comb will connect you to your roots.

Ich Liebe Dich, Meine Julienne,

Your Mutti, Suzannah

I looked around the room. The blue chairs looked darker. The front of my dress was wet, and my left hand was hurting. It had been clinching half a comb. I felt complete and filled with gratitude because my canvas was a masterpiece painted by a remarkable, courageous woman and a man who had showed me how to look at the face of courage.

She did not date the letter. There was no need to. The only need was to remember.

I picked up the telephone and called Ursula. In public I would call her Sarah.

The Canvas – A Secret from the Holocaust

A creative historical fiction, Eveline Horelle Dailey a non-Jewish author uses occupied France and the Holocaust to predispose Julienne Duprée-Fairchild's life experiences.

The turbulent and horrific era during and after the Holocaust are woven in stories Suzannah told. On a porch in her home in New England Julienne remembers the dialogues. Great love, choices people made, world travels, her marriage with Frank, the American professor in Paris, joy, and sorrow represent the colors in Julienne's canvas.

She finds the courage to explore balance in her life and finds her true identity.

Eveline calls English the language of her thoughts, French, however, is the one she spoke until her higher education began in the USA. The romance vernacular gives texture and nuance to the prose.

She writes with a voice that finds its reason in the heart of humanity.

The canvas – A Secret of the Holocaust is a novel of emotions, feelings and mystery. One reads it with tension, expecting a tour-de-force ending that Eveline Horelle Dailey delivers. With the horror of the Holocaust in the background, The Canvas is full of insights into a young girls growing up with memories of love and finding the answers to her roots.

Jasha Levi - Author of the Last Exile – Holocaust Survivor from Yugoslavia

---

Even though the book is subtitled A Secret from the Holocaust, I was caught off guard by the ending. When you discover the "secret" and then review in your mind the sequences of events, one feels even more the devastating emotional trauma. Eveline Horelle Dailey weaves throughout her novel The Canvas just as in the previous book Lessons from the Lakeside, perceptions of how the strands of our experiences are interfaced to form our own life canvas.

Mary Boehm - Boehm Design Studio

I have read and reread the manuscript. I know that our meeting was orchestrated by the Holocaust souls to implore upon you and me to keep their voices alive. I found the story to be breath taking, hauntingly beautiful, and frightening. — I am amazed at the research, accuracy as well as acumen. Your book is a must read as unfortunately there are persons who do not believe the Holocaust happened. Truth is stranger than fiction you get right into the face of your readers.

Dena Beth Jaffee — Program Manager for the Center for Senior Enrichment Through Jewish Family and Children Service at Chris ridge Senior Living Community —

The settings used by the author were not familiar to me. The way she seamlessly exposed the unthinkable kept me reading. The unpredictable ending held me motionless for a long while. Everyone should read this book because it teaches what we need to remember.

Loraine Lakey - Human Resource Professional

Eveline Horelle Dailey used her unique voice and exposes horrific events around the Holocaust. Seamlessly, she moves the reader to a place filled with love, courage and inner beauty. This is done while the main character searches for something she finds at the end of the book. Stunning!

Kathy Alto – Ph.D.

I am completely drawn in to and engaged with this story from the very first scene. The descriptions of life as it was and how hindsight creates a backdrop for action – taken and denied – keeps the reader involved with the mysteries that continue to unfold. The story of the Holocaust and its impact is shared and educates the reader in different ways – from the long-term effect of victims to the possibilities of what could have been if events were different. It makes one wonder how many other stories out there to be told are vanishing every day.

Jonathan N. Larkin

A story of coming of age and looking back to see how those around us influence and mold us. A story of love about an adult starting to understand why her important people were the way they were. Along the way, we are given little bits of what people endured during WW II. This is a book worth reading and remembering.

Delores Kramer

In this compelling story Eveline Horelle Dailey has woven a philosophy of lovingly living our lives so that forgiveness and healing are the natural outcome from the pain and suffering experiences by people on both sides of WW II.

Gladys Taylor McGarey MD. MD (H)

CONTACT THE AUTHOR: evelinenow@gmail.com

.